BISHOP ON THE ATTACK

The telephone rang and Deckard dug his way out of his thoughts to answer it. A male voice said, "Deckard?"

Deckard said, "The check's in the mail."

"Deckard, I have news for you." Deckard's scalp was tingling. The voice was flat and calm and there was a touch of Dixie in it.

"Shoot."

"This is Harry Bishop. You stay the hell away from Donna DuKane or I'll kill you. For two cents I'd kill *both* of you."

Deckard said, "Bishop, for God's sake, let me talk to you for a few seconds!"

The line went dead.

THE MISSING BISHOP

Also by Ross H. Spencer

Monastery Nightmare

Published by
MYSTERIOUS PRESS

THE MISSING BISHOP

ROSS H. SPENCER

THE MYSTERIOUS PRESS • New York

The characters in this story are fictitious, and any resemblance between them and any living person is entirely coincidental.

MYSTERIOUS PRESS EDITION

Copyright © 1985 by Ross H. Spencer

Mysterious Press books are published in association with Warner Books, Inc.
666 Fifth Avenue
New York, N.Y. 10103
A Warner Communications Company

Printed in the United States of America

Originally published in hardcover by Mysterious Press
First Mysterious Press Paperback Printing: October, 1986

10 9 8 7 6 5 4 3 2 1

THE MISSING BISHOP is dedicated to Ohio's 37th Infantry Division, the battling Buckeye bastards of New Georgia, Bougainville, and Luzon . . . the finest men I've known.

And to Shirley Spencer . . . the finest woman.

When your gal's left town and you're feeling blue
And there ain't nobody to stand by you,
When a frown don't help and a tear won't do,
Look up to the sky—maybe He knows.
When you've been kicked out of the last saloon
And the sun don't shine and there ain't no moon,
Go out on the back porch and whistle a tune
And sit there—and swat the mosquitoes.

Ross H. Spencer

1

On Saturday, July 19, 1969, Senator Edward M. Kennedy of Massachusetts announced that he had driven his automobile to the bottom of a pond near Chappaquiddick Island.

He made the front page of every newspaper in the United States of America.

On Sunday, July 20, 1969, astronauts Armstrong and Aldrin spent two and one-half hours walking on the moon.

They made the front page of every newspaper in the world.

On Monday, July 21, 1969, Kelly J. Deckard, a Chicago private investigator, was nearly mugged in the parking lot behind Mush's Teddy Bear Lounge on Belmont Avenue.

The newspapers made no mention of it.

2

It was a rotten day for Deckard, one of the worst
in recent memory. Appropriately, it was launched by
one of Deckard's bad dreams, a hell-for-leather,
technicolor affair starring Deckard and a cast of
thousands of bloodthirsty Japanese infantrymen. In
the gray of early morning Deckard struggled free of
it, piled out of bed, showered, shaved, brushed his
teeth, and looked for a fresh shirt. No fresh shirt. He
nudged Heather and asked about a fresh shirt.
Heather mumbled, "Sorry, slipped my mind." She
went back to sleep and Deckard let it go at that. He
knew the signs. Heather was skidding into another
of her moody periods. He put on yesterday's shirt,
finished dressing, drank a cup of instant coffee, and
left the house. On the front walk he planted a foot
squarely in the middle of a pile of dog manure.
Greetings from the Duncan dog across the street.
Deckard shrugged. It could have been worse. It
could have been dinosaur dung or a land mine. In his
hung-over condition he'd have noticed neither.

Halfway to the office it began to rain, a sullen,
relentless, gray downpour, and his windshield wip-

ers didn't work. Deckard rolled his window down and drove with his head poked out into the weather. He got drenched. Then the rain stopped and the sun came out and the day became unbearably hot, and so did Deckard's office. He turned on his air conditioner and it refused to respond and Deckard repaired it by giving it a swift kick in the ass, but he ripped the toe of a black oxford in the doing. By then it was time to return to the Harlan J. Woodcliffe thing.

Harlan J. Woodcliffe was well over sixty, a gnarled, white-haired little gnome of a man. He walked with the aid of a cane and he drove a flaming-red, turbo-charged Porsche. He left his Lincoln-wood home precisely at ten-thirty and Deckard followed him south to the Happy Hours Bowlium on West Diversey Avenue. In the lounge Harlan J. Woodcliffe shook hands with three elderly gentlemen and they went out to the bowling lanes. At five in the afternoon they were still bowling and Deckard went into the lounge and called Henrietta Woodcliffe. He said, "It's the same old story, Mrs. Woodcliffe. He's on his seventeenth game and he hasn't busted one-fifty."

Henrietta Woodcliffe said, "Lies! Nothing but lies! He's bribed you and you're covering for him while he's with some painted hussy in a hotel room!" Henrietta Woodcliffe had a voice like breaking chinaware.

Deckard said, "Honest injun, Mrs. Woodcliffe! He rolled six straight splits last game. He's finishing high on the headpin."

Henrietta Woodcliffe said, "You're utterly incompetent! Why, by now a *blind* detective would have caught him in bed with another woman!"

Deckard sighed. He said, "Mrs. Woodcliffe, your husband is a doddering, innocent old gentleman.

How can I catch him in bed with another woman when he's bowling at the Happy Hours Bowlium on Diversey Avenue? Alley 16. Come see for yourself."

Henrietta Woodcliffe said, "Oh, you imbecile, why do you suppose he drives that red Porsche pussy-wagon? Harlan J. Woodcliffe is an unbridled lecher, and I'm not paying you one thin dime until you've caught him in bed with another woman!" She hung up.

Deckard shook his head. Another wild-goose chase. Three days out the window. On the way to his car he noticed that the bowling party had checked out. He stopped at the desk and said, "What happened to the old duffers on Alley 16? They run out of gas?"

The kid at the desk grinned. He said, "Three of 'em did. Woody took off with a forty-year-old blonde that would knock your socks off."

"Woody?"

"Yeah, Mr. Woodcliffe, the guy with the cane." The kid chuckled. "Woody drives a turbo-charged red Porsche. Don't let that cane fool you. Woody's an unbridled lecher. You know Woody?"

"No, but I've spoken to his wife."

When Deckard went out, his right big toe was throbbing from repairing his air conditioner and a heavy rain was falling.

3

With Heather sliding into another state of depression, Deckard wasn't anxious to get home early. When Heather was right, she was very, very right, but when she was off her feed, Deckard steered clear of her. He drifted from bar to bar, stopping at Casey's Caboose and Vic Barsanto's and Lulu's Jungle Tap, among others, working his way in the general direction of his apartment, and by eight o'clock he was at Mush's Teddy Bear Lounge on Belmont Avenue. The ball game was being televised and he bet five dollars on the White Sox, who blew it in the ninth inning. The game was followed by an old black-and-white movie, something having to do with the 7th U.S. Cavalry and the Indians, starring Errol Flynn. Deckard, never a movie buff, but looking to get even, offered to bet five more on the 7th U.S. Cavalry and somebody took him up on it. Things looked just dandy in the early going, but the Indians rallied to kick the living shit out of the 7th U.S. Cavalry, Errol Flynn or no Errol Flynn; and amid the war whoops and the shouts and the whinnies and the bullets and the arrows and the blood and the dust, Georgie Treacherson buried Deckard under his customary avalanche of neighborhood gossip and a broad-beamed, orange-haired fiftyish female spilled her Tom Collins into Deckard's lap and he lost seventeen dollars playing liar's dice. Shortly after midnight Deckard slipped from his bar stool and Mush said, "Where you headed, Buzz?"

Deckard said, "Home, before a fucking python slithers in here and swallows me."

The parking lot floodlight was burned out; the night was overcast; Deckard was a couple of sheets to the wind, and he had some difficulty getting his Oldsmobile unlocked. He heard footsteps behind him and he turned to see the dull gleam of a knife at his throat. There were two men, and the tall one with pimples on his forehead and cheap wine on his breath squeezed up close to Deckard and said, "Stand easy, my friend; we just want to arrange a small loan."

The tall man's partner, a squat Latino with greasy hair, grinned a secret little grin and reached for Deckard's wallet. Deckard had always assumed that he'd slug his way out of such a situation, erupting into a human tidal wave of destruction like the television heroes, but he did nothing of the sort. Instead, he said, "Look, I have about forty dollars. Leave my driver's license, will you?"

A white Cadillac convertible came down the alley and squealed briskly into the little parking lot. The tall man lowered his knife to navel level, shielding it from view with his body. He said, "Open your yap and I'll cut your fucking gizzard out."

A big, balding man in faded blue jeans and a denim jacket climbed out of the Caddy, glancing disinterestedly at the trio standing near Deckard's car. He popped a cigarette into his mouth and headed toward the rear door of Mush's Teddy Bear Lounge, patting his pockets for a flap of matches. He stopped, turned, and walked back to Deckard's Oldsmobile. He said, "Would any of you nice people happen to have a match?"

The Latino said, "Sure, man, we got a match." His hand darted toward his hip pocket and the big man kicked him savagely in the groin before nailing the tall mugger flush on the jaw with a whistling left uppercut. It was over in a split second, with the tall one flat on his back, unconscious, and the Latino rolling around in the gravel of the parking lot, clutching his testicles, and groaning something in Spanish. The big guy plucked a Saturday night special from the Latino's hip pocket. He emptied it with knowing hands, tossing the bullets into a trash can, then threw the gun against the brick wall of Mush's Teddy Bear Lounge, where the cheap weapon disintegrated on impact. He stomped on the knife, snapping its blade off at the handle. He turned to Deckard, grinning wolfishly. He winked. "Amateurs. Lousy technique. You want some law?"

Deckard said, "Why bother? They'd be back on the streets in twenty minutes." The big man nodded and headed for Mush's back door. Deckard said, "Thanks, Mac."

Over his shoulder the big man said, "Any old time."

Deckard watched Mush's door swing shut behind his benefactor. Then he got into the Olds and drove north. A very near thing, and he'd been mighty fortunate. The newcomer had been rougher than a popcorn cob. Deckard hadn't gotten a good look at him. About all he could remember was a deep, mellow voice and the glitter of his eyes. Even in the dimness of Mush's parking lot Deckard had caught that hard, piercing glint, the same competitive flash you see in the eyes of a topflight running back. Or those of a boxer. Or those of a man who's finally caught up with the bastard who's been shacking with his woman.

When Deckard got home, he found a bill in the mail box. Northwest Florists. For the dozen red roses he'd had delivered to Heather a couple of weeks earlier. He couldn't remember the reason. Deckard didn't need a reason for sending roses to Heather. He just sent them and felt good about it.

There were two dirty dishes, a coffee cup, and some silverware in the sink. She'd had something to eat. That was good. Sometimes she went without food. He washed the dishes, dried them, and put them away.

He went into the bedroom and found her sleeping. He undressed and slipped in beside her. He kissed her on a bare shoulder. She grunted in response. That was all.

4

It was August 21, Deckard's birthday. He was
forty-eight years old. He was also six one, one-
eighty-five, dark-haired, gray-eyed, thirsty, and so
pissed off he could have bitten a chunk out of the
USS New Jersey. He sat in a creaking, gashed, black
Naugahyde-covered swivel chair at a lopsided desk
in his two-hundred-dollar-a-month office, located
directly above Joe Nitti's Italian Beef and Sausage
Emporium on West Irving Park Road, a few doors
east of Austin Boulevard, cussing a silent blue
streak. He was getting his brains knocked out by a
newfangled electronic chess opponent named Galahad IV.

Deckard wasn't the world's greatest private detective, but he was a better private detective than
chess player. He made the only move Galahad IV
had left him. He cringed like a ten-year-old waiting
for a seventy-five cent firecracker to go off.

On his desk the expensive gadget gave cursory
consideration to the last-ditch maneuver. Then it
blew its top. It cut loose with a wildly exultant
series of shrill, beeping sounds and its red lights

began blinking B6-B1! B6-B1! B6-B1! End of the line. Checkmate. Three in a row. Deckard glared at Galahad IV. Jesus Christ, how he detested that vain, gloating, know-it-all, little plastic son of a bitch!

He stuffed the chess pieces into a topless half-quart Old Washensachs beer can, unplugged the victorious device, and jammed it into the bottom desk drawer it shared with several packs of Chesterfield cigarettes, a couple of paperback novels from the Inspector Drury of Scotland Yard series, and a quart of Sunnybrook whisky.

He glanced at the perpetually ten minutes late clock on his north wall. His first appointment since Henrietta Woodcliffe was thirty-five minutes overdue. Adding those missing ten minutes made it forty-five. He'd wait another fifteen before going over to Casey's Caboose for a few birthday beers. He'd put up his sign when he left, of course. AT CASEY'S CABOOSE ACROSS STREET. Sometimes they bothered to come over and sometimes they didn't, and sometimes Deckard never knew one way or the other because when Casey's Caboose was jammed to the scuppers, he ducked around the corner to Vic Barsanto's Neapolitan Bar and he'd never gotten around to making a sign for Vic Barsanto's Neapolitan Bar.

5

Casey's Caboose was a long, low, narrow, gray-shingled frame structure wedged between a Bohemian bakery and a washing machine repair shop on the south side of West Irving Park Road. Casey's Caboose had a blue neon sign that snapped, sizzled, and popped; a badly cracked plate glass window that had never been washed; an ancient cash register that had been wired to a prizefight bell, thereby deafening everyone on the premises when Casey rang up a pitcher of beer; and a ramshackle, undulating bar that had probably been constructed within hours of Franklin Delano Roosevelt's defeat of Herbert Clark Hoover. There were a dozen or so sagging booths and a great many rickety tables where Billie Jo Spears served the specialty of the house, corned beef and cabbage. You couldn't get chili at Casey's Caboose, and you couldn't get soup. You couldn't get hot dogs, hamburgers, or ham sandwiches. At Casey's Caboose you couldn't get anything but corned beef and cabbage—half a pound of corned beef; half a head of cabbage; a pair of boiled potatoes, billiard-ball size; a hefty, rough-cut chunk of dark bread; and a quarter pound of butter. Two bucks even, including tax. Take it or leave it.

Billie Jo Spears was Casey's live-in jill-of-all-trades, the most recent in a long and dubious line. Billie Jo's predecessor had been half Comanche, half Sicilian; a husky, wild-eyed, hair-triggered damsel named Falling Leaf Stabilito, who had endeavored, not without a measure of success, to scalp a customer with a roll from Casey's old player piano, an assault that might have gone unnoticed had Falling Leaf Stabilito taken time to remove the roll from the piano.

Casey Callahan was an enormous, craggy-faced, snowy-haired sixty-year-old Irishman, stronger than a team of Death Valley mules and possessing all the charisma of an arthritic African crocodile. People traveled miles to see Casey Callahan lose his temper, and rare was their disappointment. Casey could double clutch into high dudgeon in the twinkling of an eye, and nothing, but *nothing*, infuriated him like rock music. Casey's jukebox carried melodies of Irish flavor, two or three recordings of "Toora Loora Loora," five of "When Irish Eyes Are Smiling," and no fewer than a dozen of "Galway Bay," every blessed one by Bing Crosby. Once, during the previous winter, an unsuspecting route man had cleared the machine and routinely loaded it with rock selections. When the dust had cleared, and there'd been an abundance of it, the substitute route man was flat on his back in the middle of West Irving Park Road, and so was the jukebox.

Deckard patronized several northwest-side bars, but Casey's Caboose was his favorite watering hole. Casey's was convenient, located almost directly across the street from Deckard's office; Deckard enjoyed talking to Casey; and last, but far from least, he was okayed to run a tab, a privilege that had proven convenient over the years.

The lunch hour was over at Casey's Caboose, and Billie Jo Spears was clearing the tables while Casey stood behind the bar, one huge foot up on the sink board, gabbing with Willie Clausen. Casey could have talked both arms and a leg off a statue of Calvin Coolidge, if there'd been any statues of Calvin Coolidge, and he waved Deckard a hello and dug a bottle of Old Washensachs out of his battered beer cooler. He banged it onto the bar and said, "Happy birthday, Buzz Deckard!"

Deckard said, "Thanks, Casey. It's hell to be old."

Casey said, "Me and Willie was just discussing that big rape trial back in '27."

Deckard slid onto the bar stool next to Willie Clausen's and said, "What big rape trial back in '27?"

Casey said, "The one what had good ole Clarence Darrow in."

Deckard took a swig of his birthday beer. "It's news to me."

Casey said, "Yeah, you was prob'ly too young to really appreciate it."

Deckard said, "I was six. I was damn near nine before I got interested in rape."

"Well, anyway, what happened was good ole Clarence Darrow was defending this guy which had got hisself accused of rape and good ole Clarence Darrow was cross-examining the broad what claimed she got raped, and do you know what good ole Clarence Darrow up and done?"

"I haven't the foggiest." That was a line Deckard had plucked from the Inspector Drury of Scotland Yard series.

Casey Callahan raised a words-of-wisdom forefinger. He said, "Well, what good ole Clarence Darrow done was, he hauled a bottle out of his pocket."

Deckard nodded approvingly. "Great idea! What was he drinking?"

"He wasn't drinking nothing, Buzz. We still had Prohibition back in '27."

Deckard frowned. "Yes, but that doesn't necessarily mean he wasn't drinking. Hell, in '27 my grandmother fell off a church steeple at two in the morning."

"Had she been drinking?"

"That was the consensus of opinion. What was in Clarence Darrow's bottle?"

"It was empty."

"Well, Jesus Christ, Casey, that doesn't make a lick of sense!"

"Oh, the hell it don't! Good ole Clarence Darrow jerked the cork and he give the cork to the broad what was accusing his client of rape, but guess what, Buzz?"

"I haven't the foggiest."

"Good ole Clarence Darrow kept the bottle!"

"What the hell good is an empty bottle?"

"Hey, Buzz, there's the beauty part! He tole this broad to stick the cork in the bottle; only every time she tried to stick the cork in the bottle, good ole Clarence Darrow would move the bottle! You get what I'm driving at, Buzz?"

Willie Clausen was a burly man with bushy red hair and tawny eyes that lit up like fluorescent bulbs at the first mention of sex. Willie's eyes were very bright now. He said, "You see, Buzz, what good ole Clarence Darrow was establishing was, you can't rape no broad as long as long as she keeps moving it around."

16

Deckard said, "Well, maybe they moved it around back in '27, but it's a lost art these days."

Willie Clausen said, "Oh, I wouldn't go quite that far. Mabel Crowley moves it around real good. You know Mabel Crowley. Always wears a black dress. Comes in here on Saturday nights."

Deckard said, "I don't place her. What does she look like?"

Willie thought it over. He said, "Prob'ly a steam locomotive."

Deckard said, "Oh, yeah, Mabel Crowley. I don't know Mabel that well."

"Me neither, only Les Collins was telling me. So was Harry Wentworth, for that matter. Also Angelo Fregosi."

Deckard said, "Was good ole Clarence Darrow's client acquitted?"

Casey said, "Naw, they give the poor bastard forty years. Turned out he had this broad's keester wedged in a bramble bush and she was *afraid* to move it around. Well, what I was really leading up to was, I heard all about this big rape trial when I was eighteen years old and I tole Paul Oroganoff about it."

Willie said, "Who was Paul Oroganoff?"

Casey said, "The kid next door."

Willie said, "How old was he?"

Casey said, "Eighteen, just like me. Then Paul Oroganoff went and tole Digby Farrar about it. Paul never should of done that."

Willie said, "Who was Digby Farrar?"

Casey said, "The kid what lived next door to Paul Oroganoff."

Willie said, "But I thought *you* lived next door to Paul Oroganoff."

Casey said, "I *did*. Digby Farrar lived on the other side."

Willie said, "How old was Digby Farrar?"

Deckard said, "Back to the story, for the love of God!"

Casey said, "Digby was seventeen and that very afternoon he got to thinking about it and he went and stuck his whatsis in a bottle and he couldn't pull the damn thing out."

Willie said, "What kind of bottle?"

Deckard said, "What's the difference what the hell kind of bottle?"

Willie Clausen bristled. He said, "Well, dammit, Buzz, these things could be real important!"

Casey said, "That Digby Farrar was hung like a goddam Shetland pony and the hospital had to bust the bottle on account of all the suction."

Willie's tawny eyes flared. He said, "Yeah, I see just what you mean! Sort of like a plunger, right, Casey?"

Deckard said, "Let the man finish his story."

Casey said, "Old Man Farrar lost his twenty-five cents bottle deposit."

Willie said, "*Twenty-five cents*? Man, back in '27 that must of been some kind of bottle!"

Casey said, "Yeah, Hinckley and Schmitt was madder'n all get-out! At least Hinckley was."

Willie said, "What about Schmitt?"

Casey said, "Schmitt had a coronary on the spot. All that unfavorable publicity, y'know."

Willie said, "Hey, I can just imagine!" He nudged Deckard. "Can't you just imagine, Buzz?"

Deckard said, "Silence is golden."

Casey said, "I think Thomas Carlyle said that."

Deckard said, "If Carlyle didn't say it, somebody else should have."

Willie said, "Well, personally, I got to agree with Hinckley. What about you, Buzz?"

Deckard said, "I'm inclined to go along with Schmitt."

Willie said, "What did old Man Farrar have to say?"

Casey said, "Old Man Farrar had aplenty to say. Trouble was, nobody could understand a word of it. He had his whatsis stuck in a bottle and he couldn't get it out." Casey shook his head. He said, "Jeez, them Farrars was sure strange people."

Willie Clausen's tawny eyes were contemplative. He said, "Ain't it funny the way some of them fads run wild?"

6

Casey popped for another birthday drink and Deckard sat at the bar at Casey's Caboose, watching one more of his afternoons slip unproductively away, smoking cigarettes and yawning and listening to Willie Clausen ramble on about sex. Heather had asked Deckard to pick up a quart of strawberries on his way home and that meant that he'd have to stop at Connerly's Fruit and Vegetable Stand on Lawrence Avenue. Deckard was just a trifle hesitant about stopping at Connerly's because Connerly usually had a bottle stashed under the grapes, one drink had a nasty habit of leading to another, and last summer the two of them had been arrested for throwing tomatoes at passing squad cars.

The jukebox played "Toora Loora Loora" and Casey's cash register bell clanged fiercely and Naomi Perkins busted Jake Burley in the mouth with her purse and Louise Hackett fell off her bar stool and fractured her drinking wrist and Billie Jo Spears tripped over Blind Fred Strickland's Seeing Eye dog and dropped a tray of dishes and Blind Fred Strickland's dog became very excited and bit Fat

Mary Walker in the left buttock, and all factors considered, it was a routine afternoon at Casey's Caboose on West Irving Park Road. Then the phone on the south wall rang and Casey answered it and motioned to Deckard; Deckard took the phone and said, "The check's in the mail."

The voice on the line was familiar to Deckard— flat, calm, with a slight southern twang, possibly out of northern West Virginia. "This Mr. Deckard?"

Deckard said, "Yes. Mr. Bishop?"

"That's right. Sorry I had to blow our appointment today. I was all tied up and I just couldn't get to a telephone. I stopped at your office late and I saw your Casey's Caboose sign."

"You should have crossed the street."

"I would have, but I was pressed for time. I had another stop to make and I just got home. Incidentally, I live right over here on North Marsh Street."

"What does this concern, Mr. Bishop?"

"Insurance. I have an agency on Broadway, third floor, Tradesman's Building, just south of Lawrence. Do you know that neighborhood?"

"Oh, yes, very well." Bishop's office would be in the Uptown area where a man could get laid for five dollars and have a kidney removed with a broken beer bottle free of charge.

Bishop said, "Mr. Deckard, it wouldn't be practical for me to hire a full-time investigator, so I'm looking for a man who'll work on a now-and-then basis, running down insurance claim information. Ever do anything like that?"

"No, but I believe I know the route. If Smith's disability is keeping him away from work, is Smith at home in bed or his he out painting the house. That it?"

"Exactly. What's your daily rate, Deckard?"

"A hundred, plus expenses."

"I'm unfamiliar with the scale. Is that standard?"

"It is unless you want Inspector Drury of Scotland Yard."

"Sounds fair. Interested?"

"Not if it involves the south side."

"No south side. Northwest and suburbs, mostly. Des Plaines, Park Ridge, Elmwood Park, River Grove, Franklin Park, like that. Do you have a fast camera?"

"I don't even have a slow camera, but I'm interested."

"Good! Will you be in Casey's Caboose tomorrow about noon?"

"Mr. Bishop, I'm *always* in Casey's Caboose tomorrow about noon."

"Okay, Deckard, I'll try to get by there with a camera tomorrow. If I can't make it, I'll have my wife drop it off. If you're free, there's a good chance that I'll have something for you to look into at that time."

"I'll be here."

"Excellent. I'll catch up with you tomorrow." Deckard hung up and returned to the bar. That was the way he ground out a living, a hundred here, a hundred there. A few days a month for Bishop wouldn't hurt a thing. Deckard watched Casey Callahan start into the men's room, stop short, pull back, and slam the door. Casey had turned pale and Deckard jumped from his bar stool to grab the old man's arm. He said, "Casey, are you all right?"

Casey nodded, staring with bulging eyes at the men's room door. He said, "Sure, I'm okay, Buzz, but Willie Clausen's in there!"

Deckard said, "What *about* Willie Clausen?"

Casey Callahan shook his head in disbelief. He said, "He's got his whatsis stuck in a beer bottle!"

Deckard nodded. He said, "Well, I gotta go up to Connerly's for strawberries."

7

No one seems to know how alcoholics become alcoholics. There's a theory that they're developed and there's another that they're born that way. No matter. They're here, and they're here to stay. They come in a variety of colors, shapes, and sizes, and only one in a thousand realizes that he's an alcoholic. There are no good types, but some are infinitely worse than others and the worst of the lot is the periodic lush. This one stays dry for a few days; then somebody buys him a beer and he's on his way. He gives advice to people who can't use it; he propositions escorted females; he becomes insulting; and if somebody doesn't knock him flat on his ass, he winds up his evening by getting sick to his stomach and the next morning he can't remember where the hell he left his automobile. Deckard was an alcoholic and he knew it. He wasn't a periodic drunk. Deckard drank steadily, quietly, and with maximum efficiency. He was rarely in need of a drink because if he wasn't coming back from having one, he was probably on his way to get one. It had been a very long time since he'd awakened with a clear head, and he wasn't at all certain that he'd enjoyed the sensation.

Deckard usually managed to get things done, rarely smashed out of his mind and never stone sober. He was only slightly drunk when he checked into Casey's Caboose shortly before noon, just in time to accept a telephone call. He said, "The check's in the mail."

Bishop said, "I called your office."

Deckard said, "I walked into Casey's this very second."

Bishop said, "Deckard, I just can't make it today, but my wife will be dropping in with the camera in a matter of minutes."

"Would you describe her?"

"Oh, blonde, brown-eyed, going on thirty-one, rather cute, I think. Can you run on something this afternoon?"

"Be glad to. When will I get paid?"

"Tomorrow, for sure. I'll make it a definite point to get to you then. That's the trouble with a one-man business, Deckard. I have to be seven million places at the same time."

"I know a little bit about one-man businesses. Whatcha got?"

"There's a kid on Kedvale Avenue, north of Armitage, near Palmer."

"There's *lots* of kids on Kedvale Avenue, north of Armitage, near Palmer. That's the Puerto Rican belt."

"Does that worry you?"

"Bishop, nothing worries a man who frequents Casey's Caboose on Saturday nights."

"How's that?"

"On Saturday nights Fat Mary Walker plays the

piano and Casey Callahan sings Irish songs, 'Rose of Tralee,' for one."

"What's wrong with that?"

"Well, what's wrong with that is, Fat Mary Walker can't play the fucking piano and Casey Callahan can't sing fucking Irish songs, 'Rose of Tralee,' in particular. Tell me about the kid on Kedvale."

Bishop said, "Just a minute." Deckard heard papers rustling. "Okay, Deckard, you got a pad and pencil?"

Deckard said, "No, just one helluva memory. Shoot."

"Name's Juan Salazar. He has a five-hundred-dollar-a-month sick and accident policy through my agency with Merchant's Mutual of San Antonio. He works for Koshiba Electronics in Elmhurst. Claims to have screwed up his back on the job."

"What does his sawbones say?"

"He goes along. Salazar hasn't worked in six weeks and his doc says he'll be off indefinitely."

"Then, what's your beef? You can't dispute a doctor's diagnosis."

"These Puerto Ricans play possum. I want you to nose around the neighborhood. Maybe you can shoot a picture of Salazar doing something physical."

"Such as?"

"Oh, such as arm wrestling in a gin mill or screwing his sister."

"Puerto Ricans aren't much on arm wrestling. How will I know if she's his sister?"

Bishop chuckled. "Any form of strenuous activity will do just fine, Deckard."

"Can you give me a thumbnail sketch of Salazar?"

"Sure, but it won't help a bit. They all look alike. Salazar's twenty-three, five six, about one-thirty-five, black hair, dark eyes. You're just going to have to play it by ear."

Deckard was watching a woman come into Casey's Caboose. She wore a sheer white blouse, a tailored beige skirt, and dark brown pumps. She was in the ball park of thirty, with shoulder-length, honey-blonde hair waved at the tips. She had soft brown eyes, a slightly freckled ski-jump nose, and a full-lipped, sensuous mouth. She was amply bosomed, slim-waisted, and she walked with the supple grace of a panther. She came to a slightly pigeon-toed stop and looked around. The buzz of tavern conversation dimmed to a whisper. Bishop was saying something, but Deckard cut in on him. He said, "Hold it, Bishop; your wife may be here now."

"Is she carrying a camera?"

"Uhhh-h-h, I haven't noticed yet."

"Yeah, that'll be her. Good-looking chick, but all up in the air."

"Very common condition in Chicago. I think it has something to do with the water."

"Well, see what you can do with this Salazar thing. That's 2231 North Kedvale. Got it?"

"Got it." Deckard hung up and headed for the blonde. She saw him coming and said, "Mr. Deckard?"

Deckard said, "Yes, you're Mrs. Bishop?"

She made a face. "Not really, but Harry likes to introduce me that way. My name's Donna DuKane and I live with Harry. You know how that goes."

"Do I?"

"No, not necessarily. Sorry." She dug into a large brown leather purse and produced a Minolta camera. She said, "There's film in it, Mr. Deckard. By the way, this isn't Harry's camera. It's mine."

"Thanks, I'll handle it very carefully. Care for a drink?"

Donna DuKane hesitated before saying, "Well, not this time, but thank you, anyway. I have a great deal of shopping to do." She smiled demurely and went out onto West Irving Park Road to turn left toward Austin Boulevard. Somebody whistled and Deckard found himself nodding in silent agreement.

Donna DuKane was a thoroughly beautiful woman with a thoroughly beautiful walk.

8

Kedvale Avenue was a one-way street north-bound, so Deckard turned south on Keeler to pick up Kedvale from Palmer Avenue. He drove slowly north, being extremely careful of filthy, long-haired children on stolen bicycles. If a man was out looking for trouble, he could find all he wanted on Kedvale Avenue. In that corner of the canyon a man could get his throat cut for scratching his balls.

The neighborhood was completely shot in the ass. Broken windows; flop-fendered, rusted-out vehicles without license plates; garbage strewn across ruined front yards; beer cans cluttering the streets; rats the size of beavers roaming unhurriedly from property to property in broad daylight. This wasn't creeping blight. This was galloping destruction, fanning out like a California greasewood blaze to blacken an area of more than five square miles.

There'd been a fire at 2231 North Kedvale and the front door of the house was missing. Deckard could see directly into the kitchen; the sink had been ripped from the wall. There wouldn't be a bathroom fixture or a light bulb left in the place. These people were like a horde of South American ants. What they couldn't devour they mangled, thoroughly and systematically, seemingly just for the pleasure of mangling it. Like ants, they were clannish, so Salazar would still be in the neighorhood, fire or no fire.

Deckard eased his way north to Belden Avenue, then east toward Pulaski Road. Three-quarters of a block down an alley four young men were popping a lopsided old basketball at a netless hoop nailed to a sagging garage. A possibility. Deckard checked the Minolta. Only one exposure had been used. He rolled south into the alley.

All four of them matched up with Bishop's description of Juan Salazar—early twenties, lean, black hair, dark eyes. Deckard stopped the Olds and shot several pictures through the windshield, concentrating on catching each member of the quartet at least once. If one of these cats was Juan Salazar, he'd have him by the short hair because basketball is no game for a man with a bum back.

They noticed Deckard and approached his car, grinning, chattering in shrill Spanish, one of them dribbling the basketball on the cracked pavement of the alley. Deckard slipped the Minolta under the front seat, lit a cigarette, and waited. When they reached the Oldsmobile, he opened his window and said, "Juan Salazar?"

The four exchanged knowing glances and the one with the basketball began to bounce it off the left front fender of the car. Two of them smiled greenteeth smiles and the fourth spat in Deckard's direction before hauling a small caliber pistol from a pocket. Deckard peeled rubber getting the hell out of there and his rearview mirror showed the four of them doubled up with laughter.

When Deckard swung west on Palmer Avenue,

they were playing basketball again and Deckard thought of those famous Statue of Liberty words—something like "Give me your poor, your huddled masses . . ." Deckard would have given fifty dollars to take the idiot who'd written such drivel and strand the son of a bitch on Kedvale Avenue. He'd be singing a different tune, if he got out alive.

He drove homeward and at four-fifteen he parked the Olds and sailed his hat through the door to Heather. Heather caught it and set about making vodka martinis. She'd escaped her depression and she was the Heather he had fallen in love with—cheerful, attentive, talkative, sexy, anxious to please. She made martinis until nearly nine o'clock and they went to bed at nine-thirty, gloriously drunk. At midnight they got up for grilled cheese sandwiches, black coffee, and aspirin tablets. Then they went back to bed.

This time they slept.

9

Harry Bishop wasn't at Casey's Caboose on Saturday. Or on Sunday. On Monday afternoon Deckard paged through his office telephone book, looking for a Bishop Insurance Agency and finding none. He called information, and after a long time the girl said yes, she had a Bishop Insurance Agency on Broadway. It was a new listing, she told him. Deckard rang the number. No answer. He checked the book for a Harry Bishop on North Marsh Street. There wasn't any, and this time information was unable to help him. Deckard sat at his desk, thinking about it, listening to his weary air conditioner clanking against West Irving Park Road's brassy wall of heat. It was a war of attrition and the heat was getting the best of it. The telephone rang and Deckard reached for it and growled, "The check's in the mail."

A pleasant female voice said, "Mr. Deckard?"

Deckard said, "Yes, ma'am."

"Oh, *my*, how very polite! Mr. Deckard, this is Donna. Do you remember me?"

"I don't know that I recognize the name." The hell

he didn't. He remembered her very well and he remembered her fetching, slightly pigeon-toed walk.

"Donna DuKane. I loaned you my camera. I was Harry Bishop's, well, shall we say 'paramour'?"

"Did you say 'was'?"

"'Was', Mr. Deckard. As in 'forget it.'"

"But where's Bishop?"

"In hell, for all I care. Harry doesn't live here anymore."

"What happened?"

"Harry had another iron in the fire."

"A female iron?"

"A very *special* female iron, I gathered."

Deckard said, "I'm sorry to hear that." The hell he was. Deckard's white knight of conscience was suddenly engaged in a Pier 6 brawl with his dragon of desire and the dragon had just buried its eyeteeth in the seat of the white knight's BVDs.

"Did Harry owe you money, Mr. Deckard?"

"Nothing staggering. How can I help you, Ms. DuKane?"

"Well, for openers, you might call me Donna."

"'Donna' it shall be."

"And I'd like to get my camera back."

"You can pick it up just about anytime. My office is right across the street from Casey's Caboose. I'm located immediately above Joe Nitti's Italian beef and sausage joint. Just follow your nose."

Donna DuKane said, "Well-l-l, you see, I'm at home with no compelling urge to go out into all this heat. Do you suppose you might arrange to drop it off here?"

"I can't imagine why not."

"I'd buy you a drink for your trouble."

"That would be nice. Where's 'here'?"

"Less than a mile from your office. 4222 North Marsh Street. You can come up the back way."

"In about an hour?"

"Good. Beer okay?"

"Just fine."

"I have Old Washensachs."

"That's my brand."

"Thank you, Mr. Deckard."

"Try 'Buzz.'"

"Buzz. That's cute." The smile in her voice was warm.

Deckard hung up. His white knight of conscience had ridden pell-mell into the sunset and the dragon ruled the field.

Since Heather there'd been no other woman in Deckard's life, not even a one-night stand. There'd been an incident shortly before Deckard had met Heather, one that had resulted in a certain amount of annoyance, and Deckard was waiting for that to pass. It had come at a time when he was a couple of months back on his office rent. Helen Petrakos had always collected the rent personally, and during these brief contacts they'd eyeballed each other, but neither had seized the initiative. Helen was forty-five or thereabouts, an olive-skinned, raven-haired, hot-dark-eyed, lissome damsel with a dazzling smile. She was the widow of Nick Petrakos, an immigrant Greek who'd accumulated approximately one-quarter of the business properties on the north-west side of Chicago before he'd been run over by an Ingram's Potato Chip and Pretzel truck at the corners of Peterson and Kimball.

Deckard had been suffering from a severe case of the shorts on the afternoon of her visit, but Helen Petrakos had been surprisingly sympathetic. She'd sat on the wooden chair near Deckard's desk, shifting it to face him. She'd furrowed her smooth Grecian brow and crossed, uncrossed, and recrossed her long Grecian legs until Deckard had glimpsed her lace-trimmed orchid panties a half-dozen times. She'd said that perhaps something could be worked out. She'd noted that Deckard's delinquency might be . . . well . . . completely eradicated if . . . well . . . if she knew him . . . well . . . better. . . .

Deckard had thought about it for something like five seconds before saying, "Just how well did you have in mind, Mrs. Petrakos?"

Helen Petrakos had left the client's chair, stepped to Deckard's desk, leaned over, placed her mouth on his, and plunged her tongue nearly into his throat. Then she'd stepped back and said, "That well."

The gauntlet having been thrown, Deckard had gotten to his feet, locked his office door, and cleared his desk. He'd hoisted Helen Petrakos onto the desk, stretched her out, made her comfortable, raised her blue pleated skirt to her navel, and peeled off her lace-trimmed orchid panties. He'd pulled her well-rounded bottom clear of the desk surface and he'd thrown a twenty-minute bell-ringer into his landlady.

Helen Petrakos had responded with her dazzling smile, a lingering kiss, and a receipt for two months rent. She'd stuffed her lace-trimmed orchid panties into her two-hundred-dollar leather handbag; she'd tripped lightly down the stairs; she'd climbed into her forty-thousand-dollar black Mercedes-Benz; and she'd driven away, peeling rubber for half a block, leaving Deckard staring out the window after her, wondering if he was a whore and deciding that it didn't make a great deal of difference whether he was or whether he wasn't.

Then he'd met Heather, and when Helen Petrakos had phoned, he'd manufactured excuses. He'd mailed his office rent check two weeks in advance and he'd walked the path called straight until now, but every man has an Achilles' heel and Donna DuKane had been nothing short of impressive. He'd seen her only once, and aside from raw tomcat lust, he felt nothing for her, but raw tomcat lust is a highly motivating influence and Deckard was highly motivated. He couldn't be absolutely certain of her intentions, of course. He'd have to return her camera, drink some of her beer, and see what happened, but he had precious few doubts as to how things would go at 4222 North Marsh Street. Deckard had studied the human comedy and he knew that less than half of America's sex out of wedlock springs from the honest gut desire that had raged within Helen Petrakos. He knew that the lion's share of such carrying-on is based on female spite. The average outraged woman makes a practice of turning to an associate of the man who has outraged her; it's a reflex thing. The average outraged woman doesn't take a bus downtown, get picked up by an accountant from Slippery Rock, and duck discreetly into a hotel room. Not the average outraged woman. The average outraged woman storms into the neighborhood gin mill at high noon, seizes her husband's best drinking buddy by the testicles, and drags the bewildered wretch into bed. She'll get caught and she knows it. It tastes better that way. Revenge is hers. And the recipient of her favors doesn't have the slightest idea that he's been used as a weapon.

Harry Bishop had outraged Donna DuKane. Deckard had never laid eyes on Harry Bishop, but he'd done an afternoon's work for him, and technically speaking, that made him an associate of Bishop's. It made him eligible.

10

He fished Donna DuKane's Minolta camera out of the top drawer of his old green filing cabinet. He advanced the film until it was exhausted and he dropped the cartridge for development at Sid Cohen's Discount Drugs at the corner of West Irving Park Road and Austin Boulevard. He purchased a new roll of film, installed it in the camera, and drove west.

4222 North Marsh Street was a brown-shingled two-flat, getting along in years but in an excellent state of repair. Deckard parked his Olds and followed a narrow brick walk that skirted a long, neat bed of red geraniums on the north side of the building. He opened a chain-link gate, closed it carefully behind him, and climbed the exposed rear stairs to the second-floor porch.

He saw a beach chair, a small rattan table with a yellow plastic ashtray labeled Club Williwaw, and in a copper-trimmed wooden bucket, an enormous rubber tree plant. There was a single clothesline strung loosely above the porch railing and from it dangled a white brassiere with impressive cups and

41

two pairs of white nylon panties, both sporting a great many tiny red and blue stars. Patriotic skivvies, of all things.

Deckard tapped lightly on the glass of the kitchen door and in a moment the door swung open and Donna DuKane stood there, barefooted in an ankle-length, chocolate-brown corduroy robe. She was smiling, but her soft brown eyes were bloodshot and they glistened with a blend of boiling frustration and icy fury. She said, "Please excuse my appearance. I just stepped out of the shower." If she'd just stepped out of the shower, she'd worn a cap. Her hair was perfect. Deckard extended the Minolta to her, the way a kid hands an apple to the teacher. She accepted it, nodding her thanks, and said, "I'm terribly sorry to have troubled you like this. I could have picked it up at your office. It really isn't the heat. I'm afraid I'm in a bit of an emotional state."

Deckard stepped in and eased the door shut. "I understand."

Donna DuKane shook her honey-blonde head with emphasis. She said, "No, I don't believe you do. Harry's been seeing another woman since shortly after we got together. It all came to a head on the evening of the day I brought the camera to Casey's Caboose."

"Look, Donna, it's really none of my damned business."

"Oh, of course it isn't, but it'll feel good to let off steam to *some*body!"

"All right, let 'er flicker. Who is she?"

"God knows." She locked the kitchen door and hooked the night chain, an excellent sign, as signs go, Deckard thought. "She's a shadowy figure at best, but she's real; oh, God, is that bitch ever *real!*" Donna DuKane was out of the starting gate, establishing the presence of hurt, a standard procedure. She had to be sure that Deckard appreciated the punishment she'd suffered, that he recognized this as being a period of great trial for her, and that he understood that she didn't invite virtual strangers up to her apartment every afternoon of the week. That accomplished, she'd have gained the rail and she could make the pace at her leisure.

Deckard nodded his comprehension of Donna DuKane's plight, and oddly enough, he felt that he *did* grasp the situation, fully. He could figure Donna DuKane, but he'd be damned if he could understand Heather. Well, perhaps that was for the best. No man should understand his own woman, not completely. He could remember having dismantled a kaleidoscope as a youngster. He'd ended up with an empty cardboard tube, a few chips of colored glass, and a couple of cheap little mirrors. The magic was gone. Donna DuKane was saying, "I've cried, naturally, but not like I thought I would. I could see it coming and I was braced for the impact. Anyway, it's pretty damned difficult to crack up over a man you never really possessed in the first place."

She took Deckard by an elbow to guide him toward her living room. The apartment was clean and orderly, but it looked lived in. Donna DuKane wasn't a perfectionist, but on the other hand, there were no dirty dishes in her sink. Deckard liked that. Heather kept a very loose rein on dirty dishes. To his left, the bedroom door was ajar and the bed was neatly turned back. All of the drapes were drawn and the place was dim and quiet. In the living room a big mahogany console purred a Johann Strauss waltz. Deckard sat on a comfortable tweed sofa. On the coffee table were two gleaming pilsener glasses and a chromed bucket filled with ice and several cans of Old Washensachs beer.

Donna DuKane sat beside Deckard on the sofa. She opened two cans of Old Washensachs and poured. Her chocolate-brown corduroy robe gapped open in the process and Deckard glimpsed a full, dark-nippled breast. She was a peroxide blonde; Deckard would have bet fifty dollars on it. True blondes have *pink* nipples. Donna caught his glance and her hand moved to the throat of her robe, but with no great haste, Deckard noted with approval. She raised her glass to him and said, "The best, Buzz." They sipped at the beer and Donna said, "There's no answer at Harry's office and I don't know what to do with the things he left behind. You haven't heard from Harry?"

"Not a word."

"There's a pipe and a tobacco pouch and a book of chess problems. Harry was a nut about chess. Do you play chess?"

"I play *at* it. I learned the game on troop ships. I'm no great shakes, believe me."

"I detest chess. It's so like war." The remark disappointed Deckard—clumsily obvious, smacking of something closely akin to sour grapes. He said, "Was this woman married?"

"I don't know."

"You know nothing about her?"

"Nothing beyond Harry's trumpetings about her phenomenal intelligence. Harry made a great to-do over her mind." She lit a cigarette and exhaled smoke in a thin gray plume. "It's probably better that I don't know much, I think." There was a wistfulness about Donna DuKane now.

Deckard said, "I agree. It's best that you don't have a clear focal point. Are you still in love with

Harry Bishop?" He was marking time, watching her cover the backstretch in a canter, waiting for her to make her move.

Donna DuKane threw back her head and laughed a short, bitter-sharp laugh. "In love with *Harry*? *Now*? Oh, good God, *no*! Once burned, twice shy!" She popped the tops on two fresh cans of Old Washensachs and got up to take the empties to the kitchen. Deckard watched her go. He'd always had a thing for women who walk slightly pigeon-toed. There's a certain inexplicable grace about them.

When she returned from the kitchen, they sat in silence. The stereo was on a Viennese waltz binge— "Morning Papers" and "Blue Danube." In a while Deckard said, "How did you manage to get hooked up with Bishop?"

She crushed her cigarette into an oblong white ceramic ashtray. "I didn't invite you up here to bore you with trivia."

"You won't bore me." She was coming out of the far turn now and beginning to pour on the coal.

"Well, at that time I was involved in a highly unsatisfactory live-in relationship with a local playwright who shall go nameless, at least for now. What do you know about playwrights?"

Deckard shrugged. "Not much. Most of them are gay, as I understand it."

"He wasn't gay, not *this* one, but he was crazy. I mean that. He was *nuts*, and all the more so when he was writing something. He'd stay up all night and sleep all day. He'd become detached, dark, morose. He'd talk to himself; honest to God, he would! He'd experiment with character conversation, and let me tell you, it was *spooky*, hearing this chatter at three in the morning when I knew damned well that there were only the two of us in the house!" She gave a little shudder at the thought. She said, "That wasn't all that drove me up a wall. There were two other things. He was a chess fiend. That was how he became associated with Harry Bishop; they met at some sort of chess get-together. He'd sit and solve chess problems by the hour. He even made them up himself. At these times he demanded complete silence. Christ, if I lit a *cigarette*, he'd glare at me. Anyway, once in a while Harry would come around and they'd drink beer and play chess all evening. Harry always lost; I can't remember him ever winning a game, but he was like a breath of fresh air. He'd laugh and he'd say complimentary things and he was so damned nice, and one night when Mike was in the bathroom, Harry told me that I was the only reason he ever came to see Mike and I kissed him for that, you'd better believe it! I got to seeing Harry when I had the opportunities, and eventually he offered me a way out and I grabbed at it." She shook her head puzzledly. She said, "I'll never understand this. We seemed so doggoned right for each other." She was at the eighth pole, hammering down the stretch, her words coming in heated little bursts.

"Mike was the playwright?"

"Yes. He's filthy rich."

Deckard said, "So what was the other thing that bugged you?"

Donna DuKane took a deep breath. She said, "Guadalcanal! He damned near destroyed me with Guadalcanal! When he wasn't writing or working at chess problems, it was Guadalcanal this and Guadalcanal that. He talked about it incessantly! It was a fixation with him—the Ilu River and the Tenaru River and the Matanikau River and Vandegrift and Cresswell and Washing Machine Charlie and Pistol

Pete and on and on and on, and by the time Harry took me out of there, I felt like I'd been through the whole damned campaign my*self*! Buzz?"

"Yes, Donna?"

"I'm talking too damned much. You've drifted away from me."

"No, not really." But she was right. For a handful of moments Deckard had stared from the sea at a lush green tropical island, its white beach fringed with thousands of coconut palms. He said, "Go on."

She spread her hands, palms up, in a gesture of helplessness. "Well, Buzz, that was my life with Mike—his writing, his chess, his Guadalcanal. It seemed like there should be more than that."

"But it was no better with Bishop?"

"It was better, much better, until Harry came up with Wonder Woman." Suddenly she tore vexedly at her belt and stood, facing him, her chocolate-brown corduroy robe hanging wide open, nothing under it but a rigid-nippled Donna DuKane who stared at him with unblinking, smoky-eyed challenge, and Deckard saw that she was a peroxide blonde all right because her pubic hair was jet black. There was a small, flat, brown mole on her abdomen directly north of her navel, like Tulagi in relationship to Guadalcanal. She stepped toward Deckard and the brown mole brushed his lips, and she said, "Awfully warm this afternoon, Buzz."

Donna DuKane was going under the wire, driving, and Deckard was swallowing hard. He said, "Yes, isn't it?"

She said, "I have the coolest sheets on the northwest side and the bed's already turned down."

Deckard said, "I'd noticed that." He glanced up. Her brown eyes were dilated, her nostrils flared, and she was smiling the smile of Diana the Huntress. He said, "Donna, I can't do this."

She laughed and she ruffled his hair and she locked her fingers behind his head and she crushed his face hard into her belly. She said, "Come on now, Buzz! I know why I called you and you know why you're here!" Her body was warm and slightly damp and it had a sweet, vaguely hyacinth odor, but a bevy of white knights had appeared on the horizon; they were riding hard, lances at the ready, and the dragon of desire was turning tail.

Deckard said, "No. I want to, you understand, but I *can't*."

Donna DuKane stooped to kiss Deckard on the forehead. She gave him a light pat on his cheek and said, "God bless you for that, Buzz." She cinched up her chocolate-brown corduroy robe and Deckard went out and down the stairs.

On Donna DuKane's cool sheets he'd have known it was all for spite.

11

Chicago was a busted-down whore smack-dab in the middle of her menopause. The old bat's best days were far behind her, and she knew it. Her moods were countless and born of frustration, all dangerous, all contagious. Deckard drove west through one of her more sullen periods and he found himself falling into her frame of mind. He took no pleasure in the warmth of the summer that had followed one of the most relentless winters in midwestern history. He saw no beauty in the sunset that blazed brilliant orange through black clouds piling up in the west—an artist might have praised it, but to Deckard it looked like the vestibule of hell, a prelude to an excellent evening for committing suicide with a rusty corkscrew.

Deckard was down in the mouth. He'd walked into Donna DuKane's apartment with his eyes wide open, knowing damned well what was going to happen. He hadn't committed the anticipated deed, but the fact that you shoot at a man and miss fails to diminish your original murderous intent and Deckard had left his office with designs of cheating on

Heather. He'd get over it, he knew, but at the moment his conscience was kicking up one Christ-awful ruckus and whisky would be required to soothe it.

On Gunnison Avenue he squeaked the Olds in behind a fruit peddler's truck piled with bananas and assorted melons. The sign on the tavern a few doors back said RITA'S PLACE, and Deckard thought it might be nice to talk to a woman. He didn't much give a damn if she looked like the Wicked Witch of the West; at such times in a man's life there's no company like a woman's. Sigmund Freud might have explained that; Deckard couldn't.

He left the Oldsmobile and went into Rita's Place. An oddly matched couple was just leaving the joint, a scrumptious, long-stemmed twenty-year-old blonde bit of fluff and a gnarled, white-haired little gnome of a man who walked with the aid of a cane. Deckard turned to watch the old guy pinch the maiden's sleek posterior. She squealed and gasped, "Woody, you sweet bastard!" Then she giggled and they got into a flaming-red Porsche and he drove away with his left hand on the steering wheel and his right hand up her dress. Deckard shrugged. Henrietta Woodcliffe had been right. Harlan J. Woodcliffe was an unbridled lecher. Well, more power to the old reprobate.

In Rita's Place not a bar stool was occupied and there wasn't a female in sight. Behind the bar there was a sawed-off, overstuffed swarthy man with a bright glass eye and a downright critical case of five o'clock shadow. Deckard sat at the end of the bar and ordered a double Sunnybrook with a water wash. He looked the place over and the bartender jerked his head toward a short hallway. He said, "Second door on your right."

Deckard frowned. He said, "What about the second door on my right?"

"That's the john."

"I'm not looking for the john. I'm looking for the telephone."

The barkeep said, "On the wall right behind you." He giggled. It was a strange sound, something on the order of an xylophone being played with Louisville Sluggers. He said, "If it had been a snake, it would of bitten you."

Deckard said, "If it had been a snake, it wouldn't have been on the wall."

"Depends on what kind of snake it could of been." This was one of those devil's advocates, a guy who takes the unlikely side in any discussion so long as he knows it isn't one hundred percent disprovable. He was just busting to talk to somebody about something. Apparently he'd selected Deckard and snakes.

Deckard changed the subject. He said, "Where's Rita?"

"You know Rita?"

"I may have seen her around."

The bartender grinned and pointed a stubby finger at Deckard. He said, "Gotcha by the balls! *I'm* Rita!"

Deckard studied him coldly. He said, "I think you're a different Rita." He lit a cigarette and said, "This could even be a different tavern. When a man ordered a double Sunnybrook with a water wash, Rita always saw to it that he got it."

The bartender snapped his fingers. He said, "Sorry, chief!" He poured the drink and said, "Honest to God, I'm Rita. You could even look on my license by the door. 'Samuel L. Rita,' it says. Go take a peek."

Deckard said, "I'll take your word for it."

The bartender said, "Sure. Wouldn't do me no

good to lie. You could look on my license by the door."

Deckard downed his drink and just a touch of water before pumping some change into the wall phone that would have bitten him if it had been a snake. After three or four rings a lilting voice said, "Deckard domicile."

Deckard sighed wearily. He said, "Look, Heather, do me a big favor, will you?"

Heather said, "Come right home, baby. I'll do you a favor that will drive you crazy."

Deckard said, "That's not the favor I had in mind. The favor I had in mind was for Christ's sake stop answering the telephone like that. Just say hello and to hell with all the frills."

Heather said, "Buzz, did you call just to tell me how to answer the telephone? I have all the aggravation I can handle with that darned Duncan dog crapping all over our front walk. What can we do about *that*, Mister Fix-it?"

Deckard considered the question. He said, "Well, we could go crap on the Duncan's front walk. If we wait for a full moon, maybe they'll blame it on werewolves."

"You're drunk."

"Just a little."

"Be home for dinner?"

"Could be."

"Buzz, you have a guilty sound. What the hell have you been up to?"

"Just drinking and talking about snakes with Rita."

"*Rita?*"

"Samuel L. Rita. You could look on his license by the door."

Heather groaned and hung up. Deckard pushed

his empty glass in Rita's direction. Rita poured until it ran over. He said, "This one's on me. Heard you mention werewolves. You believe in werewolves?"

"Certainly."

"You ever see one?"

"Sure."

"When?"

"Last spring."

"Where?"

"On Grand Avenue in Elmwood Park."

"Yeah? What was he doing?"

"Skinning me out of two hundred and seven dollars. The son of a bitch works for the Internal Revenue Service and Old Washensachs isn't a legitimate deduction."

"You got a gun?"

"What the hell good would a gun do? The IRS frisks everybody at the door."

"I'm not talking about the IRS. Fuck the IRS."

"I tried. That's why I was on Grand Avenue in Elmwood Park last spring."

"What I was driving at is, a man just ain't safe without a gun these days. Now what the hell would I do if a werewolf stomped in here right now?"

"Call Helen Petrakos. She could handle him."

The August storm struck with sudden, insane fury. Beyond the amber glow of Sam Rita's beer sign great gray sheets of water cascaded into Gunnison Avenue. Thunder rocketed across the heavens and blinding blue threads of lightning stitched the gloom of twilight. Sam Rita said, "Hey, good buddy, kick that door shut, if you will."

Deckard complied, and when he returned to his bar stool, there was another double Sunnybrook awaiting him. He dropped a ten dollar bill beside it. He took off his sports jacket and draped it over the bar. He was feeling better. His conscience was on the mend, and just before he'd left Donna DuKane's apartment, she'd dropped a key into his pocket and whispered, "Just in case."

Deckard said, "Hey, Sam, you got any real good snake stories?"

12

Deckard came out of a deep sleep shortly before seven in the morning. He reached for Heather. No Heather. He glanced at the bathroom door across the hall. It was open and the light was out. Heather never used an open bathroom. He slipped into his robe and slippers. He found Heather, stark naked, sound asleep on the living room floor, her blonde head cradled in the crook of an arm, her body covered with little chill bumps. On the coffee table the vodka bottle was empty and the ashtray was choked with cigarette butts. Deckard frowned. He was rarely surprised by the antics of this mercurial personality, but this was a new wrinkle. He'd never known her to drink alone.

He knelt, got his arms under her knees and shoulders, and heaved. She rolled against him, slipped her arms around his neck, and opened one badly bloodshot eye. She said, "Hello, big daddy." Her breath was sour.

Deckard said, "What was the occasion?"

No response. She was limp and out like a busted light bulb. He carried her into the bedroom and tucked her gently into bed. He showered, shaved, and dressed. He kissed her on the end of her nose. She didn't move.

Deckard made a cup of instant coffee, drank half of it, washed and dried the cup, and drove toward his office. There'd been a smashup on Harlem Avenue just north of West Irving Park Road. One lane was closed and they were sweeping up the glass and hosing down the area. Helluva place to get into a wreck, right in front of a State Police station.

The morning was heating up rapidly, and if early indications were even slightly accurate, it was going to be a bad-assed day.

13

At noon the sky was blazing cobalt and there wasn't a cloud in sight, horizon to horizon. The day had blossomed into a Class AAA smoker, one of those Chicago specials, the kind that fries your shoe soles and sautés your insteps. Deckard was in his office, preparing to put up his Casey's Caboose sign, when the telephone rang, Helen Petrakos inquired as to Deckard's health. Deckard told her it was fine, as far as he knew. Helen asked about the plumbing in Deckard's office lavatory. It was in excellent condition, Deckard told her—his brother was a plumber who inspected it almost every day. Helen wanted to know if Deckard would like to have the place painted. Deckard told her that he had a brother who was a painter and he'd take care of any painting that needed to be done. Helen asked if there were any cracks in the walls. Deckard told her that he'd noticed none, but his brother, who was a plasterer by trade, would attend to any problems of that nature. Helen wondered if the carpeting might need shampooing. Deckard said that he had a brother who was in that line of work. Helen noted that Deckard certainly hailed from a large family. Deckard said well, yes, he did, now that she'd mentioned it. Helen inquired as to Deckard's preference in lace-trimmed lingerie. Deckard said oh, none in particular, just about any old lace-trimmed lingerie would do. Helen said that she was very glad to hear that because she'd just bought a pair of lace-trimmed orange panties which she'd bring around for his approval one of these afternoons. Deckard choked on his cigarette. Helen giggled and told him that they wouldn't be in the box.

With shaking hands Deckard returned the phone to its cradle. He who lives by the sword dies by the sword. Or some goddam thing.

The door banged open and a big man sauntered in. He was a shade over fifty and he had broad, square shoulders and an obstinate jaw. His hair was sandy, what little there was of it, and his eyes were bright frosty-blue with a metallic glint. His left ear had been battered flat to his head; his nose had been broken more than once; his mouth was tight and turned down at the corners; and his hands were large, horny, capable-looking things. Deckard put him down as an ex-pug. He wore a gray, short-sleeved shirt and his brawny, bronzed left forearm bore a tattoo of a chess-set knight. His faded blue jeans sported a broad snakeskin belt featuring a huge brass buckle of the variety preferred by over-the-road truck drivers, motorcyclists, and other macho bullshit artists. He shook Deckard's hand disinterestedly and said, "Buzz Deckard?" as much in the fashion of statement as query. His voice was deep and mellifluous and it struck Deckard as being perfectly suited to the reading of romantic poetry on those radio shows that keep middle-aged women up half the night, playing with themselves—"How do I love thee?" or "The moon was a ghostly galleon tossed upon cloudy seas"—that sort of stuff. Deckard kept going back to his visitor's eyes. They had that strange flarelike quality that you tend to associate with fire-and-brimstone country evangelists and banana republic dictators, crusaders whose pilot lights are just a trifle out of whack.

Deckard nodded and said, "Where did you get the 'Buzz'? It says Kelly J. Deckard on the door."

The visitor said, "Georgie Treacherson referred me." He filled the client's chair to Deckard's left and he shifted his bulk until he was comfortable. Then he said, "My name's Mike Madison. Georgie may have spoken of me."

Deckard said, "Georgie speaks of *every*body. How is the old gossip?"

Madison made a wry face. He said, "Probably drunk, mooching drinks and meddling in somebody else's business." He looked around Deckard's twelve-by-twelve office, very slowly, his keen eyes missing nothing. He said, "Been in this location long, Deckard?"

"Oh, three years, give or take."

"I know this building. I used to go to Doc Cusimano across the hall. My bursitis was killing me."

Deckard scowled. He said, "There is no Doc Cusimano across the hall."

Mike Madison said, "Doc moved to Phoenix. His bursitis was killing him."

"How long ago was that?"

"Oh, three years, give or take." Madison smiled briefly at his own humor and Deckard found himself liking him.

It developed that Mike Madison was trying to find a man. So were the Chicago cops, more or less. Deckard received the distinct impression that it was less. He said, "Well, let's take it from the top. What's his name?"

Madison said, "Harry Bishop."

Deckard cleared his throat, dug a pack of Chesterfields out of his bottom drawer, opened it, lit up, cleared his throat again, and said, "So what about Harry Bishop?"

Madison said, "Bishop's a small-time insurance man from the Uptown neighborhood. He pulled a vanishing act last spring."

"How did the cops get into it? Are there criminal charges?"

"Nothing like that. Bishop phoned in a threat on his life just before he disappeared. There's a washed-up Chicago cop named Kevin O'Hara handling the investigation, such as it is. O'Hara's doubling in brass. He owns a honky-tonk called the Lavender Lounge down on Fullerton Avenue."

"Chicago cops aren't supposed to own taverns."

"Come on, Deckard, you know the Chicago police force. The point I'm making is that O'Hara's gin mill soaks up a lot of his time and you know the bottom line. He's just going through the motions and he'll still be investigating when Christ gets back to earth. O'Hara's over the hill."

"I'm not sure that O'Hara's over the hill."

"I've never met the man."

"Neither have I, but I've known people who did."

"What do they have to say?"

"Not much. They're dead."

"Who?"

"The Alsato brothers."

"O'Hara?"

Deckard nodded.

"He killed both of them?"

"He killed all *three* of them. Subway shoot-out at

North and Clybourn a couple of years back. Drug bust. O'Hara's a tough cop."

Madison shrugged. "Well, maybe he was, but his wife died last fall and I've heard that he isn't worth a plugged nickel anymore."

Deckard was sizing up Madison. He was wound mighty tight. He sat there ticking, almost audibly, a bull of a man with flashing frosty-blue eyes—a bad son of a bitch, if Deckard was any judge of people. Deckard said, "Bishop disappears in the spring and you start looking for him in late August. What took you so long?"

"I've been looking for Harry since he dropped out of sight, but I can't hack it and neither can O'Hara. Bishop gave the cops an address on South Cicero Avenue and I've been there. He's lived there—I've ascertained that much—but the apartment's deserted and so's his office on Broadway."

"When did he abandon the office?"

"The phone hasn't answered since he disappeared."

"Maybe he moved to Kalamazoo."

Madison shook his head. "A man doesn't pay a year in advance on an office and on an apartment and then just up and stroll into the gloaming. No way."

"A year in advance on *both*?"

"That's what they tell me."

"What sort of apartment building?"

"A roach ranch. It's managed by a drunken, cross-eyed old broad. She beat me out of a bottle of booze and tried to take me to bed. I never got inside the apartment."

"Was Bishop in the insurance game long?"

Madison said, "I didn't know he was in it at all until O'Hara mentioned it. I didn't know what he did for a living. Harry played a fair-to-middling game of chess, and that was the most interesting thing about him."

"What sort of looking fellow is he?"

"Harry was about your build and weight, dark hair, gray eyes, had a slight southern drawl; real calm bastard. You got the idea that an all-out nuclear war wouldn't have fazed him in the least."

"Well, *something* must have fazed him. You're in contact with Kevin O'Hara?"

"From time to time. I've tried to build a fire under the son of a bitch."

"Were you close to Bishop?"

"Not at all. Harry was a hard man to get next to. He was a bit of a loner."

"Why? Any ideas about that?"

"You'd have to talk to a psychiatrist. Maybe he was born that way. Hell, loners are loners. I have a hunch that you're a loner."

"I suppose that would depend on your definition of a loner."

"Loners avoid close associations like the plague. For instance, who'd really be concerned if you turned up missing?"

Deckard grinned. "Well, for starters, a whole bunch of tavern keepers would have nervous breakdowns. Bishop's into insurance. Could he have been involved in some sort of scam? Maybe a rigged claim against one of the big companies?"

Madison's steely stare drifted over Deckard's shoulder and through the south window. He said, "Not a goddam chance. Harry wasn't that bright. The only no-no he ever got mixed up in was a back-street romance."

Deckard said, "Well, don't underrate back-street romances. One of those can get a man killed in a hurry. Did Bishop use women?"

"Rather well, apparently." Madison's mouth was grim.

Deckard was being patient. He'd flush it eventually. He said, "I mean for money."

"He wouldn't have made it as a gigolo. Harry's *your* age."

Deckard said, "Well, that doesn't exactly qualify him for a penile implant." He eyed Madison. "Say, tell me something, will you?"

Madison said, "I'll try."

"Are you badly in need of a beer?"

Madison's grin was of the hand-in-the-cookie-jar variety. He said, "Yeah, I could stow a couple. Georgie Treacherson didn't tell me that you're into ESP."

Deckard said, "I'm not. It's just that you keep staring at that Old Washensachs sign across the street."

14

In Casey's Caboose Deckard led Mike Madison through a veritable jungle of wobbly tables strewn with crumpled napkins, unfinished platters of corned beef and cabbage, half-empty jars of horseradish, and scummy beer glasses. They took a booth in the rear and Billie Jo Spears showed up with a pitcher of beer. Billie Jo was closing in on sixty. She was from Hattiesburg, Mississippi, which probably had nothing to do with her face being expressionless or her incessant chewing of spearmint gum. She said, "Buzz, y'all want me to play th' jukebox?" Deckard paid for the beer and added a few jukebox quarters. Billie Jo said, "What y'all wanna heah?"

Deckard said, "Anything that won't piss Casey off." He was dead serious. An enraged Casey Callahan was an awe-inspiring sight to behold.

Billie Jo snapped her spearmint gum with great gusto. She said, "Well, offhand-like, ah'd say that 'Galway Bay' is th' big number in this heah neck of th' woods." She headed for the jukebox and Deckard directed his gaze to Mike Madison.

Madison said, "Are you booked solid these days?" He sounded hopeful that Deckard wasn't.

Deckard said, "Nothing pressing. Just trying to locate the owner of some big hairy-assed dog that's running loose out on Grimpen Mire."

Madison didn't blink. He said, "Try Stapleton near Devonshire. What's finding Bishop going to cost me?"

Deckard busied himself with the lighting of a cigarette. He didn't like the feel of the situation. When you've bitten into enough bad apples, you can spot one before you pick it. There was more here than met the eye, a nasty little undercurrent, and under different circumstances, he'd have been tempted to walk away from it, but he couldn't do that, not in this case. He owed Mike Madison something. He said, "Well, first, let's have it clearly understood that there's no iron-clad guarantee that I'll get within five miles of Bishop."

"I'm not asking for miracles. I'm asking for an honest effort."

"All right, Madison, I work for a hundred a day, but for you it's seventy-five."

Madison's growl was wary. "Don't do me any great big favors, Deckard."

"No favors. I'm just trying to square accounts. A month ago you bailed a man out of a very difficult situation in the parking lot behind Mush's Teddy Bear Lounge."

Madison's mouth sagged open. "Well, I'll be go-to-hell! Was that *you*?"

"None other."

"I remember you told me, 'Thanks, Mac.' Why did you call me Mac?"

"Just a hangover from the Marines. We called everybody Mac."

Madison's frosty-blue eyes sparkled with interest. He said, "Whoa, there! What the hell Marines? When? Where?"

"First Division. 1942. Gadarukanaru."

"Guadalcanal? You don't mean it! Why, you son of a bitch! Me, too! What outfit, Deckard?"

"Red Edson's Raiders."

"Sure, Edson's bunch! I remember you guys. You hit Tulagi and then you crossed over. You held the south end of the Ridge in September, right?"

"Right."

Madison banged the table with a big fist. "Jesus Christ, Deckard, we'll have to drink some beer over this! God! Those were the most wonderful days of my life! Why, I'd trade every damn minute I have left in return for those few months all over again! How many Nips did you knock off?"

"One, I think. I'll never be sure."

"Six, Deckard! I got *six* of the bastards! Bayoneted the first one right in the Adam's apple! He was spurting like Buckingham Fountain and his goddam eyes nearly popped out of his head!"

Deckard managed to swallow against the grain. He said, "Uhh-h-h, we were discussing Harry Bishop."

Madison plunged on. "I was with Cresswell at the Ilu. Jesus, what a helluva show *that* turned out to be!"

"Yes. Look, Madison, what about Bishop? Why this burning desire to locate an Uptown insurance agent? Where's the big rub?"

Madison came back from Guadalcanal. "Big rub? There isn't any big rub, Deckard. It's just that nobody else cares about the poor bastard."

Deckard said, "That doesn't rhyme."

Madison grimaced. "All right, Bishop was a chess pal of mine."

"Neither does that. You've yet to refer to Harry Bishop in the present tense. It's never *is*; it's always *was*. Do you think he's been killed?"

"Not *yet*."

Deckard leaned back in the booth. He said, "All right, Madison, let's have it. *All* of it, or you can deal me out."

Madison's frosty-blue eyes flashed the way they'd flashed in Mush's parking lot. He said, "You want it, you get it! My woman ran off with the bastard! Simple, isn't it?"

Deckard nodded. "So the loner isn't alone. You might call this a back-street romance."

"That's right, Deckard, and you just told me that one of those can get a man killed in a hurry!"

"Slow down, Madison."

"Slow down, my ass! I'm hiring you as a buffer! I'm giving Bishop a chance and you're his only hope! If I get to him first, he's one dead son of a bitch, so help me Christ!" Madison's big hands were trembling.

"Take it easy. This is a recent thing. You'll get over it."

"Last spring isn't *recent*!"

"You don't want Bishop dead; you want the lady back."

"Maybe so. I might give him a pass if he was out of the picture, but he isn't out of the picture and I don't have the lady back! The lady's with Harry Bishop!" Madison dug hurriedly into a pocket of his faded blue jeans and produced a roll the size of a fat summer sausage. He stripped several bills from it and dropped them onto the table. "There's a grand, Deckard! Ten days in advance, no discounts, no refunds! If you find Bishop tomorrow, keep the change!"

Deckard said, "Tell me about the lady."

"Forget about the lady! You aren't looking for the lady! You're looking for Harry Bishop! You find him and leave the lady to me!"

Deckard said, "I don't think I like your ground rules."

Madison rose to loom over the table. His smile was a chilling thing. He said, "Maybe you don't like 'em, but this is the only game in town and you'll play by 'em! I've got you coming and going! You can use a thousand bucks and your Boy Scout ethics tell you that you have to save Bishop's life!"

Deckard sat in silence, staring at the tabletop.

Madison placed a typed slip of paper at Deckard's elbow. He said, "This is all I have— Bishop's last known addresses, home and office."

Deckard nodded meekly, tucking the paper and the money into his wallet. He watched Madison swagger out of Casey's Caboose before he allowed himself the luxury of a discreet smile. Talk about your manna from heaven! Deckard felt like the stray dog when the ham fell out of the grocer's truck. He'd been in the right place at the right time and Old Lady Fate had dumped a one-thousand-dollar bonanza into his lap!

Madison wanted his woman back and he'd get her. In a few days Deckard would cough up Donna DuKane's address and Madison could carry the ball from that moment on. Deckard had tried to be decent. He'd offered Madison a rates reduction and Madison had rejected it out of hand. When Deckard had realized that Donna DuKane was the long-sought prodigal prize, he'd nearly told Madison the whole cockeyed story out of gratitude for his rescue efforts on the night of July 21. But Madison had gotten hard-nosed; he'd thrown his weight around, laid down the law, become heavy-handed and offensive, and that was going to cost him a thousand bucks. Deckard would make it look good; that wouldn't be at all difficult. In the next several days he'd make all the obvious moves. He'd check Bishop's apartment and office; he'd ask questions; he'd be goody-goody gumshoe. He'd report to Madison, and if by some coincidence he happened to bump into Harry Bishop, he'd advise him to lie low until the smoke had cleared. Then, in a week or so, he'd say, "Oh, by the way, Madison, I've located your girlfriend. Bishop walked out on her. She's living alone over on Marsh Street." Nothing to it.

According to Donna DuKane, Mike Madison was a playwright and worth a pile of money. Deckard found that hard to believe. He couldn't imagine a big, ham-handed cuss like Madison writing anything more interesting than his signature, but he was making a fancy dollar in *some* field of endeavor because he'd flashed a wad of money that would have bought a Cadillac. But Madison didn't need a Cadillac. He already had one, a white convertible, and he drove it into tavern parking lots where he kicked muggers in the balls. He was a tough, aggressive, abrasive bastard; he'd been through the mill on Guadalcanal; he'd killed a half-dozen men and relished every minute of it; and just now he was riding a foaming wave of righteous rage. He'd be the wrong man to get on the sharp edge of. Deckard would have to play it cool, but he was up to that.

He lit a Chesterfield and blew smoke at the ceiling. It had been a highly remunerative afternoon. Every so often somebody up there took a shine to Kelly J. Deckard.

15

Casey Callahan came over to Deckard's booth and said, "Who was that big, ornery-looking galoot?"

Deckard said, "Just a client who wants to retrieve some stolen merchandise."

"Heather called while you were talking to him, but I didn't want to interrupt with him throwing all that money around. He might of changed his mind."

"What did Heather want?"

"Just the usual. She was wondering if you'll be home for dinner."

"I'll call her. Did Willie Clausen get his whatsis out of that beer bottle?"

"Yeah, no problem. Wait'll I tell him about the guy who went to the tattoo shop and got his whatsis done up like a yardstick. That'll drive him crazy!"

The beer pitcher was dry and Deckard bought a bottle of Old Washensachs at the bar before calling Heather. The phone rang just once before Heather said, "Deckard domicile."

Deckard grinned. She sounded bright and chipper. He said, "Now you cut that out!"

"But, Buzz, it has such a beautiful alliteration!" She said it again, bearing down hard on the *d*'s.

Deckard said, "How come it took you so long to answer?"

"I was fighting off a rapist."

"That's nice. For a moment I thought something might be wrong. What came over you last night?"

"I haven't the foggiest. Oops! That's *your* line."

"I don't own it. I just leased it from Inspector Drury of Scotland Yard. I was surprised to find you in the living room."

"So was I. I just woke up wanting to think and drink. Angry?"

"Hell, no!"

"Are you going to be late again this evening?"

"Afraid so."

"What's cooking?"

"A client. He's short one female."

"Most of them have one too many."

"It seems to balance out."

"I'll wait up. I'll have a casserole in the oven. We'll have that and a tossed salad. Vinegar and oil?"

"Always."

"Try not to be too late."

"See you."

On a clear night Deckard's torch for Heather Ralston could have been seen in Auckland, New Zealand.

16

It was shortly after nine o'clock and the night was warm and misty. Deckard parked a few doors north of Harry Bishop's South Cicero Avenue address and stared at the building. It was right off a Dracula movie set. It came complete with swaybacked roof, creaking shutters, broken windows, and sagging steps. Deckard didn't see any bats, but somewhere a dog howled forlornly and in an alley about seventy-five million cats were throwing a sex orgy to end all sex orgies. This trip was important to his role of the hustling private investigator, but Deckard left the Olds with twinges of misgiving. He counted the steps to the building's entrance. Sure enough. Thirteen. Between the cuss words and the Hail Mary's he made it to the top without incident. Then he met Lena Goldsmith. Lena Goldsmith had been drinking and she listed heavily to port. Or it may have been muscatel. She said, "Yeah?"

Deckard cleared his throat and said, "Ma'am, are you the manager of these premises?"

Lena Goldsmith pondered the question. Then she drew herself up as high and tight as was possible under the circumstances, all of which Deckard was beginning to regard as adverse to the extreme. She said, "Who the hell elshe?" It was a fair question, but Deckard let it pass.

Lena had agate-hard, bloodshot hazel eyes, one of which was badly out of sync. Deckard wondered which was and which wasn't. She had a beak common to the backsides of old silver dollars and an underslung jaw that belonged on the front end of a 1921 yard engine. Her bosom was an intimidating thing and Deckard found himself waiting for it to blow the bodice of her ketchup-stained purple bathrobe clear the hell to Kane County.

Deckard said, "I'd like to ask a few questions about Harry Bishop."

Lena looked him over, her left eye studying his right shoulder, her right eye concentrating on his left knee. She said, "You cop?"

"Well, more or less."

"Too many copsh already."

"Then one more won't make much difference."

"Wash got on hip?"

"There's a pint of Sunnybrook in the glove compartment."

Lena smiled an alligatorish smile. She said, "Hurry back. Got water mattresh."

When Deckard returned, Lena was trying to turn her television set off. She was experiencing pronounced difficulty with the controls and the screen looked like a double order of chicken cacciatore generously sprinkled with Hupmobile drive shafts. Deckard found the right switch and Lena Goldsmith found the Sunnybrook. She sank heavily into a chair, holding the doomed bottle aloft like the Statue of Liberty's torch. She said, "Sho, wash hoppen on Harry Bishpup?"

"Probably nothing. I'm just trying to find him."

"Waffor?"

"A thousand dollars. Also to save his life. Not necessarily in order of importance. How long did Bishop live here?"

Lena counted on her fingers, lost track, and started over. After a while she said, "Shix."

Deckard said, "Six what?"

Lena squinted and said, "Shorry. Wool you repeat queshun?"

"How long was Harry Bishop here?"

"Not long ash Grampa Putnam."

"And how long has Grandpa Putnam lived here?"

Lena consulted her fingers. She said, "Grampa Putnam doan live here no more."

"Why not?"

"Move."

Deckard said, "Ah, yes."

"Grampa Putnam had aparmenn in bashemunn. Damn near drown."

"How was that?"

"Water mattresh broke."

"Think carefully now. When was the last time you saw Harry Bishop?"

"Wish time?"

"Oh, just pick one at random."

Lena uncapped the Sunnybrook and took a long blast. She surfaced for air and wiped her mouth with the back of her hand. She said, "I think I doan rememmer."

Deckard nodded. He said, "Just a moment, please." He produced a notebook and a ballpoint pen. He said, "Got to put all of this important stuff down."

Lena said. "Shurtinul! Glad be of ashinshush!"

Deckard said, "By the way, I want to look through Harry Bishop's apartment."

Lena Goldsmith peeked coyly over the muzzle of the Sunnybrook bottle. She said, "Coshya twenny."

17

Deckard took his twenty-dollar key and climbed the squeaking stairs to the second floor. The long, narrow hallway was poorly lighted and carpeted in stained, threadbare burgundy that had yet to contend with a vacuum cleaner. The walls were covered with graffiti, most of which concerned itself with the sexual practices of Lena Goldsmith's ancestors, and the air was heavy with the smell of frying onions. Deckard unlocked apartment 2-C and peered in. It was dark and silent. He stepped inside, leaving the door open while he pawed the wall in search of a light switch. He was still pawing when the lights went on and the door banged shut behind him. A tall, gangly man spun him around. He wore thick-lensed, horn-rimmed glasses; he had a prominent, pinch-nostriled nose, an Andy Gump chin, hands like hay rakes, and feet like assault boats. His eyes were feverish and he was shaking like a corncrib in a tornado. His voice was mushy and high-pitched and his words tumbled out with the frenzy of mice departing a leopard's cage. He said, "All right, Little Bo-Peep, up against the fucking wall!"

It amounted to one of those either-you-do-or-don't situations and Deckard opted for the former. They say you shouldn't slug a guy who wears glasses, but on the other hand, guys who wear glasses shouldn't go around calling people Little Bo-Peep, so Deckard busted him flush on his receding jaw with a right uppercut. He reeled across the room, his arms flailing the air like those of a berserk windmill. He crashed through a coffee table and chess pieces flew like startled birds. He bounced off a wall and came down under a tall bookcase that fell forward with a sound like thunder. Pictures fell from the walls and shattered, and for just a moment Deckard was reminded of September on Guadalcanal. He went out, closed the apartment door, and hit the stairs on the double. He passed Lena Goldsmith's apartment door the way an aging plater passes a dog food factory. He didn't once consider returning the twenty-dollar key.

He hiked to his car and drove three blocks to a Walgreen Drug Store. He found a pay phone and a directory. The Lavender Lounge on Fullerton Avenue was listed and Deckard dialed the number. A gruff voice said, "Lavender."

Deckard said, "Let me speak to O'Hara. It's important."

The gruff voice said, "This is O'Hara. What's important?"

Deckard said, "O'Hara, I have something hot on the Harry Bishop thing."

O'Hara said, "The Harry-who what the hell thing?"

Deckard said, "Harry Bishop. The missing guy who claimed he was going to be scragged."

"Oh, yeah, Harry Bishop. His buddy Madison keeps calling and demanding action. That concerned-citizen crap frosts my nuts. This you, Brizzolara?"

Deckard said, "O'Hara, there's an unconscious character up in Bishop's apartment!"

O'Hara chuckled. "Well, hell, Pete, I know that. That's Shakey Lenkowski."

"I see."

"Shakey Lenkowski was *born* unconscious. Remember when he took the sergeant's exam and got locked in the cafeteria over the weekend?"

"Fill me in."

"Damn near starved to death. Couldn't figure how to open the fucking refrigerator."

"How did he do on the exam?"

"Passed with flying colors. They got his test sheet mixed up with the Cubs' box score. I keep getting search warrants and sending Shakey up to Bishop's apartment. No way the son of a bitch can get in trouble up there."

Deckard said, "Right! O'Hara, you're a flaming genius!"

"Comes with experience, Pete. Catch you for coffee one of these mornings."

Deckard said, "Sure, O'Hara."

18

Deckard's new client caught up with him at Casey's Caboose early the next afternoon. Right in between "Galway Bay" and "Did Your Mother Come From Ireland?" Mike Madison slipped into Deckard's booth and said, "The sign on your door said you were over here."

Deckard said, "Yes, well, you see, I may have failed to mention it, but on Guadalcanal I contracted this condition. It's known as 'burnus thirstus' and it's downright incurable."

Madison said, "Man, those were the days, weren't they, Deckard?"

Deckard said, "I've had better."

"Not me. We had *men* then, not crybabies. They stood up to it, whatever the hell it was. Maybe they didn't enjoy it but they got the son of a bitch done. It's a different breed today, Deckard. Today they visit beauty shops; they wear necklaces; they go to Canada to beat the draft. Some scruffy bunch of fruitcakes!"

Deckard shrugged. He said, "Times change, Madison. The pendulum will swing back."

"Skip it. It's one of my pet peeves." Madison leaned toward Deckard and his frosty-blue eyes glittered with excitement. He said, "Deckard, I know something you don't know!"

Deckard yawned. He said, "Well, you wouldn't be driving that white Caddy convert if you didn't."

Madison said, "This is hot! Somebody else is on Bishop's trail!"

"Oh?"

"Yeah! The cops had Harry's old apartment staked out last night and some goon came in, got the manager drunk, stole a master key, went upstairs, and kicked the flaming tar out of a detective named Lenkowski!"

"Where did you scare this up?"

"I was talking to Lieutenant O'Hara this morning. I figure that the guy thought Lenkowski was Harry Bishop!"

"Did they get a description of Lenkowski's assailant?"

"Yeah! According to Lenkowski he was a goddam gorilla! Lenkowski said he stood about six eight and he weighed way the hell over two-fifty!"

"Sounds like a little too much for an ordinary man to handle."

Madison said, "Damn right! Listen, Deckard, I've done some professional boxing, but when they come that size, the average guy needs a goddam crowbar!"

Deckard said, "How's Lenkowski feeling?"

"O'Hara told me he took the day off."

"Was he hurt?"

Madison grinned. "No, he's probably out shopping for a crowbar." He motioned to Billie Jo for a pitcher of beer. He twiddled his thumbs for a few moments before saying, "You know, if this big mother gets to Bishop before I do, he could save me a nasty job."

Deckard said, "Not to mention the rest of your life in the old slammeroo."

Madison smiled like a weasel in a chicken coop. "Not on your sweet ass, Deckard! You're forgetting something they call 'temporary insanity.'"

"I'm not forgetting it. I'm just not certain that it's temporary."

Madison's eyes narrowed to hard blue slits. He said, "Are you telling me that I'm crazy?"

Deckard shrugged. He said, "Well, let's face it. A man who sits around contemplating killing a man in cold blood figures to come up a few points short in the mental health ledger."

Madison heaved an audible sigh, the kind you heave just before you explain to Junior that it wasn't nice to drop the match into Daddy's gas tank. He said, "Deckard, are you married?"

"Not exactly."

"Not *exactly*? You're saying that you have a living arrangement?"

"Today, yes. Tomorrow, maybe no. People change, Madison. You change, I change; your woman changed. It's been going on for some time now."

"Do you care for your roommate?"

"Like I've never cared for anyone in my whole goddam life!"

"All right, what would you do if some skulking son of a bitch took her away from you?"

"I'd help her pack and kiss her good-bye."

Madison snorted. "The hell you would!"

"The hell I *wouldn't*! Nothing lasts forever, but that's *all* that lasts forever."

Madison said, "Look, Socrates, stick all that old philosophy jazz in your ass! Don't sit there and tell me you wouldn't get that bastard one way or the other!"

Deckard shook his head exasperatedly. "Madison, you're operating on the premise that Bishop wants to hurt you. That's the furthest thing from his mind. He just happened to come down with a serious case of the hots for your woman. He'll get over it and so will she. These things happen every goddam day in the week."

"Not to *me*, they don't!"

"A fluctuating woman isn't worth the powder it'd take to blow her bloomers off. Any damn fool knows that."

"Boom-Boom's worth it!"

"Oh-oh! Wait a minute! Whom-Whom?"

"That was her stage name. Forget it, Deckard."

"No way I'll forget it! Did you say 'Boom-Boom'?"

"It isn't important. She used to be in show business."

"Where? Doing what?"

"Any number of places, doing any number of things, singing, dancing, acting. That good enough for you, Mr. Moto?" Madison was coming to a rolling boil.

So was Deckard. He said, "No, but it'll have to do until your wig comes down." It didn't make sense to Deckard. Two old Marines glowering at each other because of a cheapie like Donna DuKane who fluttered from bed to bed in the fashion of a bewildered gypsy moth. Boom-Boom. Sounded like a handle for a stripper.

Billie Joe brought their pitcher of beer. She said, "Y'all wanna heah th' jukebox?"

Madison found a few quarters. He said, "Here, play 'Rock of Ages' for Harry Bishop."

Billie Jo said, "Casey doan allow no rock of no kind fer no*body*." She popped her spearmint gum. "Y'all gonna have to settle fer a few 'Galway Bays'."

The beer supply had dwindled appreciably before Madison broke the silence. "Deckard, goddammit, you just don't understand, do you? A man has taken my *woman*!"

"Then she isn't your woman. She's *his* woman."

Madison said, "Not for long! Deckard, I'm not about to tell you that she's some kind of gold-plated Joan of fucking Arc. She's a tricky little minx; she schemes; she dreams; she turns herself on and off like a goddam spigot; she's gotten her life confused with some nickel-and-dime soap opera and she plays a dozen roles a week. I couldn't trust her as far as I could throw a Sherman tank."

Deckard spread his hands wearily. He was tempted to tell him where she was and go home to Heather. He said, "Madison, you've just painted a portrait of every goddam female on this planet. They're all the same. You should forget this one and catch the next train. You'll never know the difference."

"No, sir, Deckard! I know what she is, but what-*ever* she is, she's *mine*! I'll never accept this!"

"It isn't a matter of *accepting* it. It's like malaria. If you've got it, you've got it and you've got it."

"What's your fucking hang-up, Plato? You don't like this job?"

"Less and less. It's the pay that appeals to me."

Madison winked at Deckard. "You're also trying to detour a funeral."

"Yes, that's a piece of it."

"You'll never swing it."

"Don't bet the farm. I was on Guadalcanal, too."

It was the first time Deckard had heard Madison laugh. It was an unpleasant, grating sound. Madison left the booth and stood looking down at Deckard, saying nothing. His eyes were like chips of blue ice.

Then he gave Deckard a friendly swat on the shoulder. He said, "Let's not argue, Mac."

Deckard forced a smile. He said, "Okay, Mac."

"One of these days we'll talk about Guadalcanal and I'll tell you where the Nips went wrong."

"I know where they went wrong. They tangled with the United States Marine Corps."

"Right!" Madison threw a ten-dollar bill onto the table and went out, a man who was trying to regain a woman he'd never owned, a man who believed that a moody woman is an unusual woman when, in truth, a moody woman is about as unusual as a white snowball. If Mike Madison thought his Boom-Boom had been hard to understand, he should have run into Heather Ralston. Heather would have driven him into the banana bin. Heather had more moods than Boom-Boom had ever heard of and Deckard had never been able to grasp any of them.

He sloshed what was left of the beer into his glass. Mike Madison was a dedicated, possibly half-cracked, probably dangerous man, and if Deckard hadn't had the solution to the whole mess in his pocket, he'd have been concerned.

19

Mike Madison was an odd case, an overwhelming personality who steamrollered people, blithely self-assured that they took pleasure in being flattened and that they'd readily submit to the treatment whether they took pleasure in it or not. And then had come Harry Bishop, the upstart who'd promptly absconded with Madison's woman, and this affrontery had temporarily devastated the big man's ego. But Madison was an ex-Marine and he knew something of tactics. He'd regrouped and a major counterattack was in the offing. *Barely* in the offing, if Deckard was reading the situation correctly. It was easily within Deckard's powers to calm these frenzied waters, but he'd chosen to procrastinate briefly. He had a thousand dollars of Madison's money, and if he didn't earn it, he wanted Madison to *think* he'd earned it, and while he *wasn't* earning it, there'd be no harm in learning something about the man who was paying him.

Deckard found Georgie Treacherson right where he always found Georgie Treacherson. At the south end of the bar in Mush's Teddy Bear Lounge.

Georgie was wearing the same shiny-seated brown suit; he was still flushed-faced and shifty-eyed, and he was still expounding. On this occasion he'd cornered Mush's afternoon bartender, a pudgy, bald-headed man named Floyd Appleton. Georgie Treacherson was a door-to-door peddler of razor blades, shoelaces, hair tonic, and hard candies. He was a walking encyclopedia of the sporting scene, the entertainment field, and other people's affairs, particularly other people's affairs. Georgie knew who worked where, how much money they made, and how they spent it. He knew whose wife was cheating with whom and he knew why. He'd never amounted to a hill of beans and he attempted to minimize his own failures by pooh-poohing the other fellow's accomplishments. Georgie was saying, "Sure, Floyd, the Ryan kid—Betty Ryan. She got caught taking on the Lathrop brothers in Abe Dooley's van in back of the bakery last spring, and she had to screw a couple of cops to get out of it. She's Charlie Ryan's daughter. You remember Charlie Ryan. Charlie used to come in here on Friday nights after bowling. Lousy bowler. Couldn't hit a bull in the balls with a banjo. Shot 130 tops, providing he had a rabbit's foot and a pocketful of horseshoes. Charlie was on that Davis Hardware team with Lefty Denton and Joe Parker. Talked with a lisp. Sold used cars on Elston Avenue. A customer shot him over a bum guarantee. Only hit him in the ass, but he meant well."

Floyd Appleton shook his head. He said, "Only Ryan I ever heard of played shortstop with the New York Giants. Blondy Ryan."

Deckard sat on the stool next to Georgie Treacherson's and Georgie said, "Hey, Buzz, you remember Betty Ryan. Well, she just married Nick Peters.

Nick used to drive for Kleeman's Wholesale Liquors on River Road. Got to sampling his cargo and drove halfway through a chop suey joint out in Northlake. Didn't hurt anybody, but the cook went back to Hong Kong the next morning."

Floyd Appleton said, "Blondy Ryan was good glove, no hit. Sparked 'em to a pennant, though. '33, as I recall."

Georgie Treacherson said, "Yeah, John Collins Ryan. Massachusetts kid. Died about ten years ago. Real scrapper, but weak with the lumber."

Deckard said, "Scratch the Ryans and tell me about Mike Madison."

Georgie Treacherson shifted to Mike Madison without missing a stroke. He said, "Madison started coming in here a few months back. He's been down the road a piece. Rough bastard. Fought Golden Gloves under the name of Knight. That was in '36. Killed some Irish boy who called himself Kid Shamrock. Hit him after Shamrock's corner had tossed in the towel. Madison turned pro in '38, and I saw him at the Stadium in September of '40. Semi-windup. He went ten with Tiger Joe Alano out of the Bronx. Decked Alano twice in the seventh. Hell of a brawl. Alano won it on a split decision, but when it was over, Madison went out for a few beers and Alano went to Wesley Memorial Hospital for three weeks. That was Alano's last fight. It was a rematch or nothing, and Alano opened a spaghetti joint in the Queens. Didn't last long. Last I heard, he was a bouncer in some nightclub."

Deckard said, "Madison, not Alano."

"Oh, yeah, Madison. I saw Madison bust up a fight in here one night. It started over Crazy Dutch Lawson calling Bull Kennedy's wife a whore, which she is, of course; everybody knows that. They didn't want to stop fighting, so Madison cooled Lawson with a left hook and he floored Kennedy with a short right. Whole damn thing lasted about five seconds."

"Bully-of-the-town type?"

"Naw, Madison don't bother nobody, not really. Quiet sort. He was sucked up in the war and I think he got his brains scrambled. He has crazy eyes. He killed a whole mess of Japs on Guadalcanal and won a Silver Star with a cluster. Came out of the Marines and took up writing, of all things. Bona fide genius. Guess you know all about that."

"All about what?"

"Why, Madison wrote that play, *Murder Times Seven!*"

"Is that right? The one that's in the Loop now?"

"Yeah, it's been at the Ghent-Rumley on East Adams since spring, but it's been going strong in New York for damn near two years. Hot item. It may *never* close."

"I don't know anything about it."

"Well, it's just another murder mystery, but it's unique because it runs seven performances a week with seven different casts."

"Heavy casualties, apparently."

"It has seven different plots. First couple minutes of every show is exactly the same, but after that they all head different directions with a new murderer each time. On Wednesdays it's the mayor's wife and on Thursdays it's the president of the city council. People see one version, they come back to see another. It has seven times the draw potential of an ordinary play. It's a fantastic switch and it's made Madison a millionaire."

"I've never seen his name in the papers."

"You won't. He uses another tag."

"Nom de plume?"

"No, that's not it. He writes under the name of Jeremy Knight. Well, anyway, Madison took up with some young blues singer back last fall. They called her Boom-Boom. Don't remember her last name, but it had a Frenchy sound. Ace Wentworth heard her sing out at the old Club Williwaw before it burned down. Cute little blonde tomato, Ace told me, built like a row of shick brithouses. He said she could really belt a song. You remember Ace Wentworth. Moved to Idaho last month. He was a mechanic at Stutter's Buick over on Wilson Avenue. Mechanic, my rosy-pink ass! Ace Wentworth didn't know a spark plug from a fucked-up windshield wiper."

Deckard said, "Back to Mike Madison, if you will."

"He lives northwest of here. Timberwood Estates. I've been by his place two or three times. He has a statue of a knight on horseback in his front yard. Timberwood's one of those secluded places where you get an acre of weeds and more prestige than water pressure and you got to burn half a tank of gas to get to the grocery store, but the birds sing pretty providing you like crow music on account of they got some cornfields a little bit east of there." Deckard smiled and shook his head and Georgie Treacherson backpedaled. "Hey, Buzz, don't take me wrong! That's real nice country up that way." He took a Chesterfield from Deckard's pack on the bar. "But, Jesus Christ, it'd sure be one hell of a place to live during a snowstorm!"

Deckard said, "Madison mentioned you."

"Yeah, he was asking around about a reliable private detective, so I told him about you. That okay, Buzz?"

"Any old time."

"I gave you a big buildup. I told him that you're a real crackerjack. Oughta be worth a beer."

"Sure is." Deckard waved to Floyd Appleton.

Georgie Treacherson gave him a sidelong glance. He said, "It was about that Boom-Boom broad, wasn't it?"

"I can't talk about it, Georgie."

"You don't have to. Just about everybody knows she dusted him off. Dumped him for some busted-down insurance agent, the way I heard it."

Deckard didn't say anything.

Floyd Appleton brought the beers. Floyd said, "Come to think of it, there was another Ryan besides Blondy. Connie Ryan."

"Yeah, but he didn't hit as good as Blondy. Out of New Orleans. You forgot Nolan Ryan with the Mets."

Deckard said, "Also Big Joe Ryan."

Floyd Appleton said, "Who's Big Joe Ryan?"

Deckard said, "He mows the grass in the All Saints Cemetary in Marion, Illinois. Does a helluva job. Racks balls in the poolroom during the winter."

Georgie Treacherson said, "When did you meet Madison?"

Deckard said, "He dropped in at the office recently."

"Strikes me as being a bit late in the ball game to be hiring a private detective."

"Why?"

"Well, Madison was playing chess with Gary Bower. You know Gary Bower. He got a rundown music store on Grand Avenue. Now ain't that some kind of laugh, Gary Bower running a music store? Christ, Gary Bower doesn't know the difference between a woodwind and a goddam hurricane!"

"What about Gary Bower?"

"Gary got the impression she's been gone since sometime in the spring. You give a nightclub dame that kind of head start and she could be selling her ass on Boardman Street in Youngstown, Ohio, before you got your horse saddled." Georgie took a slug of his beer. "You ever been on Boardman Street in Youngstown, Ohio?"

Deckard said, "Not that I can remember."

Georgie Treacherson said, "Then you've never been on Boardman Street in Youngstown, Ohio." He rolled his eyes. He said, "Baby, you'd remember."

Floyd Appleton said, "Hey, ain't there a catcher named Mike Ryan with the Phillies?"

20

Deckard drove thoughtfully homeward, Belmont Avenue west as far as Harlem Avenue, north to Foster Avenue, and then back to the east a couple of blocks, through smoky August twilight and top-volume rock music billowing discordantly from rusty Chevrolets haphazardly driven by unwashed children with kinky hair and scraggly moustaches. He was weary and half-looped on beer. When you got right down to it, Deckard wasn't really crazy about beer. Its taste wasn't particularly appealing, and ten or twelve bottles made him dull and gave him morning-after headaches that were genuine bastards. Deckard blamed the chemical preservatives and whatever the hell else they dumped into the stuff and he drank it anyway, quite often in prodigious quantities because it went further than whisky and in the middle-going it served to relax him and make him affable, even slightly talkative, and he enjoyed this phase.

There was a lostness about Deckard; he'd been born with it. He'd never honestly felt that he really belonged anywhere with anybody. His few close associations had amounted to interludes soon terminated by lengthy introspective spans overflowing with emptiness. Mike Madison had sensed this and he'd hit the nail right on the head. Deckard was a bit of a loner, but Heather Ralston had helped tremendously.

Heather was tempermental, often given to strange stretched-out periods of silence. Her highs were too high, her lows too low, and she vacillated till Deckard was half out of his mind. She wasn't a strong woman and she had a distinct tendency to march with the band that played the loudest. She was desperately in need of being cared for, and this was good for Deckard. He needed that feeling, it was all-important to him, the knowing that he was her crutch, her shield and buckler. Heather loved Deckard, or she seemed to think she did, and not having a satisfactory definition of love at his fingertips, Deckard hadn't pursued the subject to any great lengths. He'd taken what Heather had been willing to give; he'd been grateful for it; and he'd concentrated more on what he felt for her than on what she felt for him.

Since they'd shared his three-room garden apartment, their relationship had lost little of its original luster. They had a relaxed alliance save for Heather's mysterious moods. Deckard tried to avoid her during these periods, granting her opportunity to work things out for herself, and there'd been times when the process had required days.

When at the top of her game Heather was an outgoing person, and they held a great many wavelengths in common. They shared a keen appreciation of the ridiculous, enjoying silly poetry and strange cartoons and claiming to believe in unicorns. They laughed a lot and sometimes they sang together because Heather carried harmony beautifully. They drifted into long discussions of nothing in particular and they arrived at no conclusions worthy of mention, the talk being simply for the purpose of exchanging ideas, however farfetched. Deckard knew a great deal about Heather Ralston, and he knew nothing at all. There'd been milestones in her life and she'd spoken of a few, but for the most part, she was vague about her past. She was obviously well-read, but Deckard had never seen her open a book. She'd committed long passages of Longfellow's "Hiawatha" to memory, but she seemed uncertain as to when she'd learned them. She prepared dishes that were completely foreign to Deckard and he teased her about them, declaring that he wasn't about to eat something he was unable to pronounce, but he ate them and they were delicious, and when he'd ask her where she'd picked up her culinary skills, she'd tell him that she really didn't remember.

The best and worst of their times came in bed because Deckard never knew which woman he was going to bed with. There were three of them. There was the woman of ice who yawned, turned her back to him, and went right to sleep; there was the passive woman who submitted to his thrusts without the slightest response; and there was the unabashedly passionate, no-holds-barred, frantic, clawing woman, the one who commanded him to *do* something, do *any* damned thing, but for *God's* sake, do it, *do* it, do it *now*—the bundle of raw sexuality requiring infinitely more than he'd ever been capable of delivering. When that third woman was through with Deckard, he'd apologize for his lack of endurance and Heather would laugh and assure him that he was God's gift to womankind and they'd fall asleep, her fingers locked with his and her hot, tight, damp little rump snuggled to his belly.

They added up to something far better than Deckard had ever experienced. He'd never laid claim to being an authority on women, in or out of bed, but he'd been from the barnyard to the chip yard and he recognized quality when he saw it. What mattered to Deckard was his glad anticipation of being with her again, even if she'd gone no further than the bathroom, and this, or the lack of it, spelled out the value of any relationship. Or so Deckard saw it.

He opened the door to his apartment on North Miriam Avenue and peeked in, hat in hand. Heather was ready, standing in the middle of the living room, clad in skintight baby-blue shorts, skimpy white halter, and spike-heeled white pumps. Her hands were on her hips, her long legs ever so slightly spread, her green eyes dancing, and she was grinning her saucy, capped-teeth grin. She stuck out her tongue impishly before saying, "Come on, Buzz, throw the damned thing!" Deckard faked once, twice, and sailed his hat in her direction, frisbeestyle. Heather plucked it deftly out of the air with practiced nonchalance. She gave Deckard a self-important little wink and said, "That's eighty-one out of what? Ninety-three, isn't it?"

Deckard said, "Huh-uh. Ninety-five."

"All right, split hairs, but it's still one hell of an average!"

"Better than eight-fifty. Just wait until they make hat-catching an Olympics event."

Heather said, "You bet your ass!" Deckard closed the door and took her in his arms, all he really had or wanted in this great big, ornery world. He kissed her. She smelled awfully nice. He sniffed and she didn't appear to notice. He sniffed again, this time very audibly, and she said, "I heard you the first time. It's *Reverie* by François Carrieré."

Deckard said, "I can't afford *Reverie* by François Carrieré."

"Cheap stuff, honest!"

Deckard shrugged. "Okay."

"You're a pushover, Buzz."

"I know it."

Heather brushed a stray lock of copper-gold hair from her forehead with one hand while pushing Deckard toward the sofa with the other. She smiled, "Beer or martini?"

"No beer. I'm full of beer." He kicked off his loafers and slumped down into the sofa. He plunked his feet onto the coffee table and watched Heather go into the kitchen, spike heels clicking pertly on the tiled concrete floor. He watched her make the martinis, admiring the firm bounce of her bosom as she manipulated the shaker. When she brought the drinks, Deckard said, "Baby, you shook all over."

Heather's smile was cunning. She said, "Oh, dear God in Heaven, *all* over?"

"*All* over."

"I'm glad you were watching."

"So am I."

"Do you always watch?"

"Every damned time."

Heather clinked glases with him. She said, "Do I look good when I shake all over?"

Deckard whistled, low and long, and Heather kissed him. It was a slow, cool, wet-lipped, martini-flavored kiss. He said, "You know how good you look."

Heather stared at him, suddenly sober-faced, nodding. She said, "That's right, Buzz. I know."

Deckard had some trouble disconnecting his gaze

from the deep V under her white halter. When he managed to wrench it free, he leaned back and sighed.

Heather said, "Rough day?"

"Somewhere between rough and rotten."

"Bushed?"

"Heather, I'm getting old."

"You'll never prove it by me."

"A beautiful lie from a beautiful woman."

They worked on their martinis and Deckard studied her with undisguised admiration. She watched him devour her with his eyes, absorbing his appreciation like a blotter. She said, "Did you find the woman you're looking for?"

"Yes, back in March. She uses cheap perfume."

"Tell me."

"It isn't a woman; it's the man who took off with the woman. No, I haven't come across him. If he walks up and introduces himself, then I'll have him."

"You're not all that interested in him?"

"Oh, I'm interested, but I'm not losing sleep over him. I can resolve this thing whether I find him or not."

"That's good." Heather scooted close to Deckard on the sofa. She put her lips to his ear. She whispered, "Are you in the market for a bit of action?"

Deckard said, "Heather, you'd better believe it!"

Heather nodded. "I caught your vibes." She rose, half-smiling an all-knowing smile. She undid her white halter and draped it over the coffee table. She squirmed her tight baby-blue shorts to the floor and stepped free of them to stand naked in her white pumps. She straddled Deckard's lap, facing him, her knees on the sofa. She was smoother than whipped cream and her breasts jutted like pink-tipped rockets. She cupped them and thumbed the nipples to rigidity. She said, "Ooo-oo-o, Buzzer, so am *I*!" She caressed herself, her eyes wide and unseeing, her tongue darting back and forth across the moist velvet of her lips, her hands slipping downward and across her navel to the crisp hair at the cleft of her thighs. She gasped, "Check me, Buzzer! Am I ready?"

Deckard checked her, below and beyond her fingers. Heather winced, grabbing Deckard's shoulders, sucking in her breath sharply. Deckard said, "You'll never be readier."

Heather said, "I could have told you that fifteen minutes ago!" She stood, bending to take his hands, and tugged urgently on them. Her eyes were sparkling, molten green. She was the third woman now, the woman who writhed in bed, the demanding and insatiable woman, the woman who was everything a woman should be, everything that most of them aren't. She said, "Buzz Deckard, come with *me*!"

Buzz Deckard complied.

21

The August morning was hot and Deckard mopped sweat as he eased past Lena Goldsmith's door and up the stairs to Harry Bishop's old apartment. The building was quiet except for the merciless rape of "Ramona" by a first-floor accordionist. "Ramona." The name spirited Deckard back over a great many years. Once, in those dear, dead days beyond recall, there'd been a high school dance. There'd also been a Ramona Dickerhoof. God, but she'd been homely! Ramona Dickerhoof would have frightened a vampire out of a blood bank. She'd glued herself to Deckard until the band struck up "Goodnight, Sweetheart." Deckard had dropped out of school the next morning and Ramona Dickerhoof had gone on to become a very big wheel in the Women's Liberation movement. It figured.

He rapped on Harry Bishop's door. No response. He knocked loudly and said, "Commonwealth Edison inspector!" He stepped back and waited. If Shakey Lenkowski opened that door, there was just no telling what might happen. Deckard stood there, listening to silence. Then he took out his twenty-dollar key, unlocked the door, and kicked it open. No Shakey Lenkowski in evidence.

He went in and began to look around. The coffee table lay on its side, two legs snapped off, a chess board on the floor and chess pieces dotting the faded blue rug. Books were scattered in every direction and Deckard noticed an old volume on chess by Capablanca. Glass from the shattered pictures sparkled along the lengths of two walls. Deckard entered the bedroom. The bed was unmade and the sheets were filthy. Hardly the proper setting for the seduction of a fair maiden. Or even Ramona Dickerhoof. He opened dresser drawers and found them as empty as the bedroom closet. He checked the kitchen. Some plastic dishes, a few pieces of cheap dining ware, a pair of coffee cups, a dented frying pan, and the like. He opened the refrigerator door and the odors of rotting foods nearly drove him to his knees. He slammed the door, gagging. It was a smell that never failed to transport him to Bloody Ridge and some seven hundred Japanese bodies swelling and festering in the searing Solomon Islands sun.

On the sink board there was a stubby briar pipe, its contents half-smoked to fine ash. Under a badly scarred kitchen table he saw a dead mouse in a trap, dried to a bit of grayish fluff. He checked a nearly empty wastebasket and found another trap behind it, this one baited with withered cheese, still unsprung. Deckard popped it with his foot. He had no overwhelming love for rodents, but there was something about traps that he liked even less.

He returned to the living room and went through the spilled books. Apparently Harry Bishop was a Western-yarn buff. Aside from the book by Capablanca the entire library consisted of the writings of Zane Grey and Clarence E. Mulford. Deckard shook each volume vigorously, hoping to dislodge a scrap of paper bearing a name, a telephone number, or an address. No dice. He surveyed the wreckage of the coffee table and he looked at the chess pieces. They were expensive, intricately hand-carved. He could understand a man leaving a pipe behind. Bishop might have owned a dozen like the one on the sink board, but a classy chess set should have been the first thing into a suitcase. Maybe the set hadn't belonged to Bishop. Shakey Lenkowski might have brought it along to help kill the stakeout hours. Doubtful, Deckard thought. He just couldn't associate Lenkowski with chess. Cribbage, perhaps, but not chess.

The living room closet offered nothing but a badly torn black nylon windbreaker with "Greene Park Chesnuts" in white script flocking across its back. Deckard went through the slash pockets of the garment. He found a few chunks of coarse tobacco and a folded piece of paper. On the paper was a chess problem:

The drawing was crude, and below it, in block print, were the words, "White to move and mate in three." Deckard gave it a brief glance before stuffing it into a shirt pocket. He'd never solved a chess problem in his life, but Galahad IV ate them for breakfast.

Deckard left the shabby apartment, locked the door behind him, and went down the stairs quickly and quietly. He drove northward through the sullen late-August heat, the soft, steady roar of his air conditioner dulling the tumult of South Cicero Avenue traffic. What an utter gold mine of information! After going through that apartment, Inspector Drury of Scotland Yard would have yawned and driven directly to Harry Bishop's new quarters. Well, Buzz Deckard wasn't Inspector Drury of Scotland Yard, not by one helluva long shot, but his yawn was effortless. He really didn't give a Tinkertoy whether he found Bishop or not, but now he'd be able to tell Madison that he'd checked the apartment. Another few days of this farce and he'd tip his client to the address of Boom-Boom or Donna, her current moniker, and Madison would huff and puff and threaten to exterminate everybody in sight, but he'd do no such thing. He'd make an impassioned visit to 4222 North Marsh Street and maybe he'd persuade her to return to Timberwood Estates and maybe he wouldn't, but either way, Deckard would have a grand of Madison's money and Harry Bishop would be out of danger and everything would be just hunky-dory.

Sure, it would.

22

Mike Madison came into Deckard's office about one o'clock that afternoon, lugging a twelve-pack of Old Washensachs beer. It wasn't the same Madison who'd walked away in a bit of a huff a day earlier. This Madison was bright-eyed and bushy-tailed, all sweetness and light. His peace banners were flying and you could have sliced his cordiality with a busted soup ladle. He said, "Hi, Mac! How're they hanging?"

Deckard said, "I get 'em twisted in revolving doors." He pushed Galahad IV to a corner of his desk.

Madison said, "I get the same problem on merry-go-rounds." He grinned. "I thought we might gab about good old Gadarukanaru a bit."

"It's been a while."

"Yeah, twenty-seven years ago yesterday we shot up the *Asagiri*, the *Yuguri*, and the *Shirakumo*. Twenty-seven years ago tomorrow we shot down fourteen Nip planes."

"What happened twenty-seven years ago *today*?"

"The dehydrated spuds turned sour. I kept a diary.

107

Well, pop a couple of tops and we'll compare notes. Hello, what's this?" He was staring at the chess problem. "Looks like a white-to-move-and-mate-in-three thing."

Deckard said, "Yeah, I found it on a scrap of paper in a jacket pocket at Bishop's apartment a few hours ago."

Madison shook his head. "It's obviously contrived. No man on earth could honestly maneuver himself into a fucked-up situation like this. Never in ten million years."

"I just set it up. I haven't had time to study it."

Madison guffawed. "It doesn't *require* any study, Deckard. You want the solution?"

"No, if I can't figure it, I'll feed it to Galahad."

There was a big green fly roaring around the office, the kind that sounds like a pissed-off B-52. It buzzed Deckard and he made a retaliatory swipe at it, missing by two feet. Madison turned away from the chess problem, parked in the client's chair, and opened a can of Old Washensachs. He said, "At what level do you play that electronic dumbbell?"

Deckard frowned. "Dumbbell? Why, that plastic bastard beats me three out of five at Intermediate level."

"Give you five-to-one I can whip its ass at Tournament level in twenty minutes."

"Some other time. Right now I have Harry Bishop on my mind."

"Good boy! Any progress?"

"Slow track. Bishop's jacket had 'Greene Park' lettered on its back. Greene Park's a playground just south of Evanston. I'll get up that way. There might be a connection."

Madison nodded. "He won't come easy. This is one helluva big town. Speaking of chess, Harry wasn't too bad at it. His offense lacked imagination, but he threw up a well-organized defense. Harry was rated a shade better than eighteen hundred."

"How does eighteen hundred stack up with your rating?"

Madison smiled. "Not well at all. I can be shooting for a Master's any time I put my mind to it."

Deckard said, "By the way, Bishop left an expensive chess set in his apartment. I can't see a dyed-in-the-wool chess enthusiast doing that."

"Maybe it wasn't Bishop's set. Maybe it belonged to the cop who got coldcocked."

"Unlikely. Lieutenant O'Hara told me that this cop gets locked in cafeterias."

Madison glanced up. "You've talked to O'Hara?"

"Briefly, on the phone. He got me mixed up with another guy."

Madison said, "That figures. Honest to God, Deckard, the Chicago police force is right out of the Katzenjammer Kids! So, how about Guadalcanal? Great sport, wasn't it?"

"Great enough to hold me for the rest of my fucking natural life!"

"Remember August 21 on the Ilu?"

"I remember August 21 anywhere. It's my birthday."

"Ichiki's 28th Infantry staged an all-out banzai attack from the west bank. Christ, it was beautiful, the way we butchered those bastards! We counted over eight hundred bodies and God knows how many died later!" Madison's frosty-blue eyes were blazing and he was laughing uproariously. Deckard watched him with awe. Madison could just as easily have been discussing a tug-of-war at a Sunday-school picnic. He'd really *enjoyed* the carnage! Madison

109

said, "The Nips weren't ready for canister shell. You've seen what canister can do to a man."

"Yeah, I wish I could forget some of the things I've seen. That's one of them." It was time to swap subjects. Deckard said, "Look, Madison, I'd like just a little more information on the Bishop matter."

Madison shrugged. "You've already got all I can give you, a couple of addresses and a description. What more can I do?"

"You can tell me about Boom-Boom."

Madison's frosty-blue eyes grew hostile. "What *about* Boom-Boom?"

"What's her full name?"

Madison busied himself with the opening of two fresh beers. Without looking up he said, "What the hell's the difference? How can that help you?"

"If she's with Bishop and I happen to find her, then I've got Bishop. Do I have to draw you a diagram?"

"Maybe she isn't 'Boom-Boom' these days. If she's back in show business, she could be 'Little Red Riding Hood' or 'Mademoiselle Flambeau.'"

"Why would she go back into show business?"

"To support that rotten son of a bitch Harry Bishop, that's why!"

"Is that likely?"

"I didn't say it was likely; I said it was *possible*. Look, I don't want Boom-Boom bothered."

"It isn't a matter of bothering Boom-Boom; it's a matter of finding Bishop."

"Will you promise to keep her out of it?" Suddenly Madison was like a child pleading for the safety of a puppy and Deckard saw himself as an axe-wielding barbarian running amok in an old people's home. Still, he had to establish himself as being Johnny-at-the-rat-hole, anxious to pounce on any possible lead. He said. "Madison, how the hell can I promise to keep her out of it when she's already *in* it up to her ears? Jesus Christ, Mac, you didn't leave *her*; *she* left *you!*"

"Come on, Deckard, you know what I'm driving at! No scenes, no excitement, no trouble for her! She's a very sensitive woman!"

"Also just a trifle on the balmy order, according to you."

"Okay, okay, so she's missing a few marbles. So who plays with a full deck these days? Boom-Boom's bright, she has adequate depth, and she was damned good for my writing."

It was Madison's first reference to his literary career and Deckard grabbed at it. "Do you write?"

"Not since Boom-Boom left me. I'm locked tighter than a Polack's strongbox. I haven't hooked two words together in months."

"So tell me about her. It might be good for you."

Madison sighed resignedly. "She was billed as 'Boom-Boom LaTreuse, Queen of the Blues.'"

"She sang blues numbers?"

"She sang any goddam thing. She could bust an audience wide open with 'Fascination.' She sang, and maybe once in a while she'd strip if one of the regulars didn't show up. There's nothing wrong with that, Deckard. She was just filling in."

Deckard said, "I didn't say there was anything wrong with it. The best stripper I ever saw was saving her money so she could send the Pope a solid gold cross."

"Maybe LaTreuse was her real name; maybe it wasn't. I never knew her by any name but Boom-Boom. I met her at a place called the Club Williwaw. Then I lost track of her for a while, but I found her again. She's from Galion, Ohio, and Jesus Christ, Deckard, do we *have* to talk about her?" Madison's face was buried in his big, horny hands and he was sobbing like a three-year-old.

Deckard said, "Sorry, Mac." He meant it. But the questions had been obvious, and if he hadn't asked them, Madison would have wondered why. Rather lamely Deckard said, "Every little bit helps."

Madison jerked out a red bandana handkerchief. He dried his face and blew his nose noisily. He said, "She's my woman, Deckard! She's my woman yesterday, today, and every damned single step of the way to the cemetery! She's *mine*, goddammit!" There was a thick silence. After a long time Madison emitted a short, harsh chuckle. He said, "Deckard, I'm a fucking cradle-robber. I'm old enough to be Boom-Boom's father."

"Age doesn't matter if the relationship works."

"It worked. It was ticking like a Swiss watch until Harry Bishop came along." His frosty-blue eyes were bloodshot. He said, "Deckard, I just have to kill that dirty bastard!"

Deckard said, "Well, that'll be a big fucking help, I'm sure. You'll do time in Joliet and Boom-Boom will find herself a new boy. Use your goddam head!"

"Then find Bishop and get him the hell out of my way because, so help me, he's running on borrowed time!"

"Do you have a picture of Boom-Boom?"

"I don't believe in pictures. There's never been a picture that didn't break *some*body's heart." The big green fly rocketed out of nowhere to sizzle northward under Madison's nose. It zoomed to the ceiling, peeled off, fell into an impressive Immelmann, and made for Madison a second time. Madison's left hand shot out with a speed that amazed Deckard. He caught the fly and crushed it slowly. He dropped its tattered remains to the floor and he rubbed his smudged palm on a knee of his faded blue jeans. He said, "That's how a professional does it, Deckard! You let him romp a bit and then you kill the son of a bitch!"

Deckard opened two more beers and Madison accepted one, nodding his thanks. He was calm now. Apparently the incident of the big green fly had satisfied something within him. He said, "That's how I want to go, Deckard—quick. That fly was lucky. We might not be so fortunate, you ever think of that?"

"Yes, I've thought of it."

"I'm sorry I didn't get it on Guadalcanal, fast, right between the eyes, on the last day of the campaign. Hell, there's never been anything like Guadalcanal for me. It was a tonic, an elixir; I *lived* on Guadalcanal!"

"The closer to death, the closer to life?"

"Yeah, something like that, I guess. But there could be one big moment left for me, Deckard. That'll be when I pump a slug into the sneaking four-flusher who stole Boom-Boom." He got to his feet and said, "See you around." He went out, closing the door softly behind him, leaving Deckard slumped, limp as a rag, in his swivel chair. He felt like he'd gone through a meat grinder.

There was no longer the slightest doubt in Deckard's mind: Mike Madison was fully capable of murder. He'd killed a Golden Gloves opponent; he'd wiped out six Japanese infantrymen; he had a single-track mind and it was focused on Harry Bishop. Given the chance, he'd kill Bishop the way he'd killed the fly, and with fewer regrets. In Madison's book Harry Bishop rated exactly the same immunities granted a Jap soldier on Guadalcanal. None whatsofuckingever. Madison was at war.

And private investigator Kelly J. Deckard had a deranged client. He should have known it the very minute he'd learned that Madison was a writer. Writers are usually cuckoo, to one degree or another. It was a firm trade requirement. He dug a can of Old Washensachs from Madison's twelve-pack and opened it. What would happen if the truth surfaced, if Donna DuKane told Madison that Deckard had worked for Bishop prior to Madison's contact or if Madison told Donna DuKane the name of the detective who'd spilled the beans? Plenty, if it happened, but it wouldn't. If Donna went that far, she'd be running a strong risk of Deckard telling Madison that she'd tried to take him to bed, and how else would Deckard know about that black mole north of her navel? If she went back to Timberwood Estates, she'd do it with her mouth shut. And Deckard saw no chance of Madison revealing that he'd hired a detective. Madison would take complete credit for the tracking job. It would be good for his ego and it would serve to discourage future safaris on the part of Donna DuKane alias Boom-Boom LaTreuse.

Deckard sat there, swilling beer, wishing to Christ that he'd avoided this kettle of rotten fish as his instincts had advised at the outset. But now he was in it up to his ears and he'd just have to brazen his way out of it. Well, he'd done that before, more than once, but never when involved with a client the likes of Mike Madison, prizefighter, war hero, millionaire playwright, and big green fly hunter.

23

The beer just wasn't hacking it for Deckard. He took out his bottle of Sunnybrook and nipped at it, sprawled in his swivel chair, feet up on his desk. What had happened to Mike Madison shouldn't happen to Buzz Deckard, yet he knew there was an inevitability about it. Sooner or later Heather Ralston would slip away from him, or he from her—the law of averages indicated an eventual division. In a world crammed with losers why should he be an exception? Ultimately, everybody loses everything, and there *are* no exceptions. Though the mills of the Gods grind slowly, yet they grind exceeding small. Or words to that effect. Well, if he was going to lose Heather, he was going to lose her and that would be all there was to it. He'd never employ Madison's tactics, chasing a woman in hopes of catching up with her and changing her mind. What's done is done and there's nothing in the past but ashes.

The office door opened and a burly man entered. He wore a sweat-splotched gray gabardine suit, a white sports shirt, and scuffed, down-at-the-heels black loafers. He had receding black hair combed straight back, and his dark, intelligent eyes were wide-set above a pugnacious nose and a belligerent, no-nonsense jaw. He walked directly to Deckard's desk, shoved out a strong, stubby-fingered hand, and said, "Deckard, I'm Detective Lieutenant Kevin O'Hara from downtown."

Without saying a word Deckard handed him the bottle of Sunnybrook. Without saying a word Lieutenant Kevin O'Hara accepted it. He kicked Deckard's door shut, tilted the bottle, and drank deeply. He placed the bottle on the desk and said, "Thanks." He lowered himself onto the client's chair, leaned back, and crossed his legs. He handled himself with great confidence, Deckard thought. He said, "Deckard, there's a minor pain-in-the-ass matter we may be able to help each other with."

"The Bishop business? Mike Madison said you were on it."

O'Hara smiled. "Yeah, I haven't been moving fast enough to suit Madison. He mentioned that he'd hired you."

Deckard said, "Well, there's a reason for Madison's fervor. Harry Bishop buzzed off with his chickie."

"Uh-huh, then that explains it. Madison's been driving us nuts. Calls three, four times a week. You making any headway?"

"Nothing worthy of mention. You?"

"Zilch. Bishop called the department last spring and said somebody had phoned and threatened to kill him. It was probably Madison who called to make the threat."

"No. Madison's really hot. If he'd been that close to Bishop, he'd have closed in."

"Well, by Chicago standards it was a run-of-the-mill thing until Bishop sideswiped a squad car early last week and blew the scene of the accident."

"How did you trace him? License number?"

"What the hell license number? He was running without plates and there's been no driver's license issued in his name. We got a description of the car and we found it abandoned down on Garfield Boulevard."

"With no plates how did you know it was Bishop's car?"

"There was a bill of sale in the glove compartment. Nice car except somebody had pulled the radio. Gray '68 Buick Wildcat with red pin-striping and all the gingerbread. Bishop bought it cash from a woman named Minnie Murdock over in Schiller Park."

"You talk to her?"

"Hell, no, we can't find *her*, either. Her address on the bill of sale doesn't jive. There is no Klinger Street in Schiller Park. There's a chance that the Murdock broad sold Bishop a stolen vehicle. We're checking that angle."

"How was Bishop's address listed on the bill of sale?"

"South Cicero Avenue. The rent on the apartment was paid way the hell in advance, but Bishop hasn't been in it since Christ was a corporal."

"Bishop's between the devil and the big blue pond. Madison's out to kill him and the police want to lock him up."

O'Hara said, "We'll lock him up when we find him, but that Madison stuff is all malarkey. I've heard that kind of crap before."

Deckard said, "Don't bet your shirt. Have you met Madison?"

"No, and not at all anxious to."

"Well, take it from me, Madison has a few loose rivets. He's a savage. Hell, he killed a kid in a Golden Gloves bout."

O'Hara's eyes narrowed. "When?"

"Back in '36, they tell me. He was fighting under the name of Knight."

"Who'd he kill?"

"Some Irish youngster who called himself Kid Shamrock. Madison turned pro and was doing pretty well until the war. He was with the First Marine Division on Guadalcanal and he won a Silver Star with a cluster. Don't sell this bastard short. He's over fifty, but he's a couple hundred pounds of dynamite."

"Well, look, Deckard, if you're convinced that Madison may kill Bishop, why the hell are you helping him find the poor bastard?"

"Helping Madison isn't the idea. The idea is to get to Bishop and tell him what he's up against."

"That's a little more like it." O'Hara pulled a cigarette from a crumpled pack and popped a wooden match with his thumbnail. He said, "Who's the bimbo Bishop hauled ass with?"

"Some ex-nightclub twister they called Boom-Boom LaTreuse, Queen of the Blues. How does that handle grab you?"

O'Hara stared at the floor, dragging on his cigarette, letting smoke trickle from a sardonic half-smile. He said, "Right by the gee-whillikers. I'll bet forty-five dollars she can't sing her way out of a wet paper bag."

"One guy told me that he'd heard she was pretty good. She used to work at a joint called the Club Williwaw."

"Yeah, it was out on Milwaukee Avenue beyond Wheeling. It burned down and it's just an ordinary little gin mill now, but it used to be a real turned-on establishment. She wouldn't have needed a helluva lotta talent to work at the Williwaw. At the Williwaw all that mattered was how fast they could skin out of their panties. About this Madison, what does he do for a living?"

"He writes plays."

O'Hara snorted. "Doesn't everybody?"

Deckard said, "Sure, but Madison hit the jackpot. He has something called *Murder Times Seven* running in New York *and* in the Loop."

"That's Madison's? It's at the Ghent-Rumley on East Adams. My sister saw it. Scared her half out of her drawers. She told me it comes in seven different packages. So Madison's a celebrity."

"He wrote it under the name of Knight, I understand."

"Same name he fought under? Christ, after he killed somebody as Knight, you'd think he'd have dropped it."

"He has a thing for knights. He has a chess knight tattooed on his arm and a guy was telling me there's a statue of a knight on horseback in his front yard out in Timberwood Estates."

O'Hara shrugged. He said, "Well, whatever." He reached for the Sunnybrook and studied the label. He said, "You know, I've always been partial to this booze. Good stuff, but it may be the name as much as anything. It has such a nice, clean sound." He drank and said, "Well, Deckard, this is a nuisance thing, but I'm stuck with it. If you come up with a break, give me a jingle, will you?"

"Be glad to. Maybe you can put Bishop where Madison can't get at him."

"We'll take a shot at it. Can't have people driving around tearing up municipal property, can we?" He drank again and returned the Sunnybrook bottle to the desk. He said, "I own the Lavender Lounge down on Fullerton Avenue, little bit east of Albany. Drop in some evening and I'll square up with you."

He went out, leaving them alone—Deckard and his empty bottle.

24

According to Mike Madison, Harry Bishop was approximately Deckard's size, age, and coloring. Madison hadn't gone into pinpoint detail, but Deckard was assuming that Bishop was of average demeanor and appearance. If he'd been a loudmouth or a flashy dresser, Madison would have mentioned it. If he'd been particularly homely or handsome, Madison would have harped on it. So Deckard was looking for a man with two arms, two legs, and no visible saber scars, and Deckard might have tripped over him a dozen times without being any the wiser.

Chess had been the bond for Bishop and Madison, and at some point in their string of get-togethers Bishop had encountered Donna DuKane, then known as Boom-Boom LaTreuse. Something had clicked between them. There's no explaining that sort of magic, but everyone has experienced it at least once, even as Deckard and Heather Ralston had known it in their first hours together. Call it chemistry or rapport or wavelength harmony or predestination or what-the-hell-ever, it works and it never fails to lead to a darkened bedroom.

Madison might have sensed this linkup. He might have bided his time in the belief that it would run its course and fizzle out. If he had, he'd been very wrong. The spark had been fanned to a blaze and now the fat was in the fire.

There's nothing unique about a man vowing vengeance upon a knave who makes off into the night with a fair damsel; Deckard had known a dozen similar cases, but murder most foul is a horse in another race. What little remained of Mike Madison's sanity was dangling by the slimmest of threads, and one glimpse of Harry Bishop was apt to send him off the deep end, ass over tin cups.

Deckard wasn't exaggerating the situation; he was merely looking it in the eye. Madison was an ex-prizefighter, and that spoke volumes. To amount to more than a ripple in the ring a man must be imbued with a desire to hurt people; and Madison hadn't stopped at inflicting punishment—he'd *killed* a man. Throw in a stretch on Guadalcanal and half a dozen dead Japanese soldiers, one bayoneted in the throat, multiply by an unfaithful mistress, add a double-crossing chess buddy, mix thoroughly, and you have on your hands one extremely unstable explosive just waiting to go bang.

Two more days, that would be enough. Two more days and Deckard would announce that he'd found Boom-Boom LaTreuse living alone at 4222 North Marsh Street under the name of Donna DuKane. Then he'd go back to quiet office mornings with Galahad IV and Inspector Drury of Scotland Yard. He'd handle simple divorce cases; he'd spend his afternoons at Casey's Caboose, drinking beer, soaking up "Galway Bay" and Willie Clausen's interminable ramblings about sex, and he'd go home in time for dinner and he'd make love to Heather Ralston in his own inimitable substandard style. Life would be simple again. Then, perhaps in October, they could take a few days and drive to Lebanon, Pennsylvania, because Heather was from Lebanon and she'd spoken often of how she'd like to go back to walk those smoky-blue autumn hills in the hush of early evening. Heather was a rank romanticist and Deckard found pleasure in indulging that which he didn't fully understand. By Deckard's calculations, yesterday was gone and tomorrow might never get here, so it all came down to today and doing the best you could with the son of a bitch.

25

It took Deckard nearly an hour to find the old Club Williwaw. It stood at the edge of a small gravel-topped parking lot on the east side of Milwaukee Avenue, a mile or so north of Deerfield Road, considerably less than half its original size, a mere ghost of its gaudy, bawdy predecessor. The small portion surviving the fire had been boarded and aluminum-sided and the sign above the door said JAKE'S JOINT. Deckard parked next to the only automobile in the lot, a sparkling-new Chrysler New Yorker with its right front fender freshly crushed in.

Jake's Joint was a quiet, immaculately clean place. It had a subdued country music jukebox, three booths, and six tables with red and white checked cloths and black plastic ashtrays. It had a fifteen-foot bar and a six-foot-six, glowering, kinky-haired bartender who told Deckard that his name was E.P. Unumberto. Halfway through his bottle of Old Washensachs Deckard said, "What's the *E.P.* stand for?"

E.P. Unumberto looked around guardedly. He leaned over the bar and lowered his voice. He said,

"The *E* don't stand for nothing, but the *P* is for 'Pluribus.' It was my old man's idea. He was drinking at the time."

Deckard nodded his sympathy. He listened to the jukebox play "Steel Guitar Rag" and "You Only Want Me When You're Lonely." It was a welcome relief from a steady diet of "Galway Bay" and "Mother Machree." Not that Deckard had anything against Mother Machree. He'd always figured her for a nice old broad.

Deckard learned that E.P. Unumberto had worked in the building for more than fifteen years. He'd been one of the four night-bartenders when it had been the swinging Club Williwaw, but now he went it alone, four in the afternoon until two in the morning, six nights a week. He said, "It ain't much, but it beats hell out of going to work." He wiped the back bar and added, "I think."

Deckard said, "What kicked off the fire that finished the old Williwaw?"

E.P. frowned. "Nobody knows for certain, but it was probably internal combustion. We had us some red-hot articles in those days."

"You must have felt like a leopard that gets a job in a meat market, all that lovely young snatch buzzing around."

E.P. shrugged. "That's what everybody thought, but it wasn't that way at all. I talk to five, ten guys like you every damn day. They come in here with an arm-load of memories of how things used to be and they want to know was I jazzing this floozie or did that floozie like to be greeked." He shook his head. "Man, I don't even remember their *names*, let alone what they did in bed! Why, them tramps went through here faster'n a double dose of salts. Over the years there must of been four, maybe five hundred of 'em, singers that couldn't sing and dancers that couldn't dance. They generally lasted something like two weeks, tops. Some of 'em wanted to go to Broadway or Hollywood; some of 'em was looking for sugar daddies—and *all* of 'em screwed. Most of 'em was selling it on the side, and if they wasn't selling it, they were giving it away out in the parking lot. They all sort of blend together in my mind, if you know what I mean."

"None you can recall clearly?"

"Oh, sure, there was some I'll never forget, but the Good Lord knows I've tried."

"Like who?"

"Well, we had one that had an ambition to make like one of them radiator-cap ornaments you used to see on the old LaSalles and Pierce Arrows. You know what I'm talking about?"

"Yeah, I've seen them."

"They was broads with big boobs and they was all arched out into the wind with their arms extended and their hair flying straight back."

Deckard nodded. "Packard had a dandy. Looked like somebody had goosed her with a porcupine."

"Well, this broad kept talking about it until some drunk took her up on it and she finally got it done."

"You don't mean it."

"Hell, yes, I mean it! Happened right after we closed, about four in the morning! She climbed onto the hood of his car, stark raving-ass naked, and away they went, sixty-miles-an-hour right down fucking Deerfield Road!"

"I'm a dirty son of a bitch!"

"Hey, that's exactly what the Deerfield Police Chief said when he seen them twenty-five trucks in the ditch."

"What the hell happened?"

"Well, what the hell happened was she was going east and that military convoy was headed west."

"What was her name?"

"Slips my mind, but I'm pretty sure it got in some of the newspapers."

Deckard ordered another Old Washensachs and drank in respectful silence. After a while he said, "Do you remember a cute little blonde blues singer named Boom-Boom LaTreuse?" He didn't care if E.P. Unumberto remembered her or not. This trip was a grandstand play for the benefit of Mike Madison. Deckard would tell Madison that he'd located Boom-Boom by talking to people at the old Williwaw.

E.P. stood, scratching his jowl puzzledly, the way you scratch your jowl on Sunday morning when you're short eighty-two dollars and you've just found a size 46 girdle in the backseat of your automobile. He said, "Funny thing. There was a couple Chicago cops in here asking about the same bimbo."

"When was that?"

E.P. glanced at the Old Washensachs clock on the wall. "Little over an hour ago."

"Guy named O'Hara?"

"Yeah, but O'Hara wasn't driving." E.P. slammed the bar rag into the sink. "It was the skinny one with the mad scientist glasses! He backed that goddam black fucking Ford into the fender of my brand-fucking-new Chrysler New fucking Yorker."

"I noticed that fender."

"His name was Lenkowski. He shouldn't be a cop. He should be with Ringling fucking Brothers fucking Circus! You know Lenkowski?"

"We've met, very briefly. What about this Boom-Boom LaTreuse?"

E.P. squinted. He said, "Blues singer? Blues only?"

"No, not exclusively."

"There was one who sang 'Fascination' better than average, but she was a stripper. You're looking for a singer."

"I think she did a little of both."

E.P. drummed the bar with his finger tips. "Blonde cookie. Sang 'Fascination' just before she peeled. Helluva body. Tits that stuck out like oh-my-God. From Ohio someplace."

"Galion?"

"I don't recall what town, but that's the tootsie you're looking for, I'll bet a sawbuck."

Deckard dropped a business card and a ten-dollar bill onto the bar. He said, "You win."

"I got no idea which direction she went from here, but I'll talk to some of the old customers. One of them may of seen her around."

Deckard said, "Give me a call."

E.P. was gazing glumly into the parking lot. He said, "Don't run into my automobile if you can help it."

Rolling south on the tollway, Deckard found himself wondering if there was a Hall of Fame for private detectives. If there was, he figured he'd be in it someday.

On a visit.

26

The bedroom was dim, illuminated only by the pinkish glow of the streetlight on the parkway. Deckard was completely exhausted. He made mention of this to Heather. He said, "Heather, I'm completely exhausted."

Heather said, "Poor baby!" She ran her fingertips lightly over Deckard's forehead. She said, "Golly, Buzz, you're sweating up a storm!"

Deckard said, "I have given my all in a noble cause."

Heather's soft laugh skittered through the bedroom. "Sir, you were nothing short of magnificent!"

"Yea, verily, woman, thou hast given credit where credit is due."

Heather's voice sobered. "Buzz, it isn't the sex that's wearing you out; it's this running around looking for a man you wouldn't know from Don Juan."

"Yes, I would. Don Juan would be the guy with his cock in his hand."

"Be serious, damn you!"

Deckard said, "All right, I'll be serious. I don't

131

believe this matter is quite as bad as it looks, but it's a helluva lot worse than it appeared to be at the beginning. The guy I'm looking for ran away with my client's woman and my client wants to kill his ass."

"But you can stop him?"

"I think so. He'll settle for getting his woman back, and I've found the woman."

"Where?"

"No matter."

"When?"

"Before I met my client.

"How can that be?"

"Coincidence."

"Is she pretty?"

"Very."

Heather sat up cross-legged on the bed. She studied Deckard. The rosy blush of the streetlight filtered through trees to weave leafy patterns on her creamy body. Deckard placed a hand on her knee. He felt that he could have looked at Heather Ralston for a thousand years without blinking once. She found a cigarette and Deckard watched the match-flare gleam and die in her green eyes. She said, "Buzz, why don't you just ditch the whole crazy mess?"

Deckard said, "I'll ride it out for another couple of days. Then I'll tell him where she is."

"Why two days? Why not now?"

"Because now's too damn soon. I want him to think I've done a bit of work for his money."

"What do you think will happen when he finds her?"

"I think he'll forget about the man and concentrate on getting her back."

"But won't that lead to a dangerous confrontation?"

"No, the lady lives alone now. She was dumped."

"What if she won't go back with your client? He'll probably be furious."

"To put it very mildly."

"Then he'll hit the warpath again. Can't the police protect this man from your client?"

"They can't protect a man they can't find. This guy did a number on a Chicago squad car, and he was driving without a driver's license and plates. The cops are trying to round him up. They were just an hour ahead of me on a lead I ran down this afternoon."

"Do you honestly believe your client would kill him?"

"There's a chance."

"Is your client capable of killing?"

"He's capable of it. He's no stranger to violence. He was a prizefighter and he was a war hero. He's an emotional, tightly wound man. Oh, yes, he's up to killing somebody, depend on it."

"Who is he?"

"That's unimportant. The police know who he is; that's what counts."

"Buzz, I don't like this situation at all. Why don't the police take your client into custody?"

"On what the hell charges? He hasn't killed anybody and he'd deny that he intends to. He uses me as a sounding board for all his blood-and-thunder talk. He seems to take a perverse delight in laying in on me."

Heather put her cigarette out and said, "Buzz, how do you feel about Chicago?"

Deckard said, "I've seen places I'd rather be."

"Name them."

"How much time you got?"

"All right, if you don't like Chicago, why don't we just pack up and move? We'll start over."

"Start over doing what, for Christ's sake?"

"I don't care. You're in a sleazy, risky business. We'd find something decent somewhere."

"In Lebanon, Pennsylvania?"

"No, Lebanon's just for remembering. We could move out west."

"Great! I'll become a gunfighter."

Heather swore.

"Bronc-buster?"

After a long silence Heather said, "Buzz, I don't want to have our baby in Chicago."

Deckard sat up like a jack-in-the-box and they were nose to nose. He said, "*What* baby?"

Heather reached to rumple his hair. She said, "Now don't get all excited."

"I'm not all excited! I'm all paralyzed!"

"Sweetheart, it isn't going to happen right away."

"Oh, you're goddam right it isn't going to happen right away! How's about three or four Halley's comets from now?"

"I've dreamed about us having a baby."

"So have I! Heather, they call those things nightmares!"

"Just one, Buzz! You and me! *Us! Ours!*" Deckard stared at her in wide-eyed amazement. She was serious, by God! Well, it was temporary; he was sure of that. It hadn't been two weeks since she'd suggested that they buy a canoe, paddle to Australia, and write a book about the trip. When he'd told her that it would probably be a very short book, she'd wanted to know what had happened to his spirit of adventure. Compared with this tangent, the canoe idea had genuine appeal.

Deckard said, "Come on, Heather! You're pushing

thirty-one and I'm working on forty-nine. We'd be in wheelchairs before the kid got around to shooting heroin!"

"Buzz, ages are only numbers."

"Well, I don't know what those numbers do to you, but they scare the living bejesus out of *me!*" Deckard sagged back to his pillow and covered his eyes with a forearm.

Heather sprawled beside him on her flat, taut belly. She said, "Will you do something for me?"

"Anything. Anything but *that*. Name it!"

She nuzzled his ear. "Will you think about it? Just *think* about it?"

Deckard sighed. He said, "Heather, no babies."

She giggled and moved very close to him. She said, "Big boy, anytime I want your baby, I'll *get* your baby." Deckard didn't respond and Heather kissed him. She whispered, "Some night I'll show just how easy it'll be."

Deckard lay there, groping for sleep. He felt the bed begin to quiver with Heather's silent laughter. He grinned and said, "You rascal!" He pulled her to him and kissed her cheek. His lips came away salty. She hadn't been laughing.

Heather and her flights of fancy.

27

Deckard sat in his office, half smiling, shaking his head, doing his damndest to decode Heather Ralton. Once in a while he thought she was crazy. Most of the time he was certain of it. The woman lived on pipe dreams. She made sudden turns to adopt strange stances. At one moment she was the supremely confident mistress of her own destiny; at the next she became the somber-eyed fatalist, completely vulnerable to Kismet's every whim. But there was a single thread of consistency. Regardless of her outlook, she was ever the face-to-the-wind, onward-and-upward, profoundly philosophical gothic novel heroine, and Deckard knew that he was watching a first-rate actress who was applauding her own performance. And Deckard had become a bit of an actor himself, professing to accept Heather's role of the hour as the real Heather Ralston when he knew damned well that there *was* no real Heather Ralston, that she amounted to a constant stream of thespian assignments, all played in Heather's Little Theater of Misty Romance. Deckard had gladly made this concession because he wanted her, whoever she was, because he adored her, and because she needed him.

It stood to reason that bearing a child would be near Heather's heart, if only in fantasy. She'd told Deckard that she'd suffered a miscarriage in Lebanon, Pennsylvania. She hadn't made a particularly big thing of it; she'd mentioned it, casually enough, in one of her sentimental moments. Deckard had said that he was sorry and Heather had chewed on her lower lip, stared into space, and noted that life was like that. Deckard had agreed that it was; they'd had vodka martinis and the miscarriage hadn't been mentioned since. Apparently, she hadn't enjoyed a tremendously happy marriage. Its sole redeeming feature was the fact that it hadn't been tremendously *un*happy. It had survived, she'd told Deckard, simply because it hadn't died, and she'd added that this was how it was with most surviving marriages, and Deckard had thought it over and observed that he wasn't at all sure she was right but that he was willing to take her word for it.

Heather and her husband hadn't tried again for parenthood. They'd just gone along, working and saving money, and working and saving more money, until he'd suffered a fatal heart attack from worrying about all the money they'd saved. When he'd died, Heather had been sorry because he'd been a good man, if dull and unimaginative, and she'd left Lebanon for Chicago, and Deckard knew the rest of it, and what the hell, Buzz, why look back? Deckard had said that she had the right idea because looking back didn't change anything, and neither did looking ahead for that matter, and they'd had more vodka martinis and switched subjects. Deckard didn't appreciate hearing about her life with Eddie Ralston. The thought of Heather with another man disturbed him and Heather had seemed to sense this, and their chats became confined to their own relationship.

The telephone rang and Deckard dug his way out of his thoughts to answer it. A male voice said, "Deckard?"

Deckard said, "The check's in the mail."

"Deckard, I have news for you." Deckard's scalp was tingling. The voice was flat and calm and there was a touch of Dixie in it.

"Shoot."

"This is Harry Bishop. You stay the hell away from Donna DuKane or I'll kill you. For two cents I'd kill *both* of you."

Deckard said, "Bishop, for God's sake, let me talk to you for a few seconds!"

The line went dead.

Deckard hung up, very slowly. Sweet Jesus Christ on a clear blue Galilee morning! You try to save a man's life and he promises to kill you! Good old Harry Bishop!

Maybe Madison had a point, after all.

28

Deckard had stopped at Sid Cohen's Discount Drugs to pick up the prints from Donna DuKane's Minolta camera and now he climbed the rear steps at 4222 North Marsh Street. He found Donna DuKane on the porch, wearing her chocolate-brown corduroy robe, parked in her beach chair, reading a bright-colored paperback novel, and exposing a g odly amount of smooth, tawny thigh. She peered at him over her book and said, "Well, I thought I'd never see you again."

Deckard said, "Oh, I've been hither, thither, and yon."

Donna said, "How was everything in Yon?"

"Just about the same. They have a new mayor."

She shook her head in mock exasperation. She said, "I bare my body to a man and he walks out. I give him the key to my apartment and he doesn't use it. That could make a woman wonder about her sex appeal."

Deckard said, "Donna, believe me, there's nothing wrong with your sex appeal."

"Harry called me this morning. He wants to come back."

"He called *me* half an hour ago. He wants to kill me."

"For what?"

"Visiting your apartment. How did he know?"

"I told him. I said that I'd shoved it right in your face and you'd turned it down. Harry's upset. Wonder Woman lit out for the tall timber with a country singer."

"Musical beds."

"Yes, isn't it? It's good to see you. Won't you come in? I don't leave for work until six."

"You're a working girl?"

"Just one night a week, downtown."

"Doing what, may I ask?"

"Well, primarily, hoping for broader and brighter horizons." She got to her feet and stepped to her laundry-line to remove the clothespins from a pair of white panties flecked with little red and blue stars. She winked at Deckard. "Did you ever think you'd see a full-grown woman stand on her back porch and take her panties down?"

Deckard said, "Not in broad daylight. Where's Bishop? I want to talk to him."

"If it's about money, forget it. Harry's a deadbeat. I don't know where he is, Buzz. He pleaded for another chance and I laughed at him. He threw a tantrum. Harry was an only child. He's very good at tantrums."

"Does he have a gun?"

"Yes, a snub-nosed, foreign-made thing. There were times when Harry carried large sums of money."

Deckard followed her into the kitchen, appreciating her slightly pigeon-toed walk. He sat at the

142

kitchen table and she brought him a can of beer. She poured herself a glass of lemonade from a frosty pitcher and sat across from him. Deckard said, "You aren't drinking?"

"Never on work days." She lit a cork-tipped cigarette with a small, gold-plated lighter. "But I *smoke* on work days." She blew smoke at him and stuck her tongue out, wiggling it. "And I do any number of other things. Want a demonstration of my versatility?"

Deckard skirted her offer by fanning the Minolta photographs on the table. He said, "I took these pictures in an alley between Kedvale and Keystone. One of these guys may be Juan Salazar."

Donna ignored the shots of the Puerto Ricans and picked up the first picture in the series. She studied it, grimacing. "Ah, yes, I'd nearly forgotten this one."

Deckard played it dumb. He said, "Is that Bishop?"

"Oh, no, this is dear, sweet, lovable, even-tempered, chess-crazy, Guadalcanal-happy Mike Madison."

"Who?"

"Mike Madison, the playwright I left for Harry. Out of the frying pan and into the blast furnace."

She handed him the picture. Mike Madison, clad in a black tuxedo with a red cummerbund, was kissing a laughing, waving Donna DuKane on the cheek. Donna wore a form-fitting violet gown and she held an enormous mixed bouquet. Deckard said, "What was happening?"

"Just a party. Incidentally, Harry snapped that picture, long ago." She rose from her chair, gathered up the photographs with a quick swooping motion and pitched them into a cabinet drawer, slamming it shut with an air of finality. She said, "Those were happier days."

Deckard said, "Would you happen to have a picture of Bishop?"

Donna DuKane spun like she'd just been stung by a hornet. "If I'd ever had one, I'd have burned the damned thing! Why do you ask?"

"Just wanted to check out your taste in men."

Donna returned to the kitchen table, placing her palms on it, leaning in Deckard's direction, and looking him full in the eyes. She said, "Well, Buzz, let me tell you about my taste in men. Recently it's undergone a thorough overhauling. Why, just the other day I had a gentleman up here and I did my damndest to coax him into bed, but he kept his pants on and do you know what? I *admired* him for that. He's an honorable man, and I think it's high time I met one of those!"

Deckard said, "Honor had nothing to do with it. I came up here to take you to bed. I wanted you so badly I could *taste* you."

"All right, taste me *now*, dammit! I just douched!"

"Donna, I'm living with a woman that I'm crazy about. She's built a wall that I just can't climb!"

"I'll tell you what you're doing. You're living with a woman who has you sexually intimidated. She's younger than you, right?"

"Yes, eighteen years, give or take."

"How old are you, Buzz?"

"Forty-eight, going on seventy-five."

"Then I'm *nineteen* years younger than you."

"I never was much on calculus."

Donna DuKane came around the table to seize him gently by the ears. She said, "I won't intimidate you. I can send you home with a feeling you aren't getting at home. Give me a chance! You'd like it, Buzz."

Deckard left his chair, disengaging her hands. "I know damned well I'd like it—I'd *love* it—but I can't *do* it, dammit!"

"You can't *do* it? You won't have to move a muscle! Just stretch out on my bed and I'll ride that damned thing until it turns *purple*! You can soothe your conscience by putting it down as rape! Come on, Buzz, last one in bed is a sissy!"

Deckard was hanging on by his fingernails. He said, "Donna, haven't you ever felt that you *belonged* to someone?"

She peered at him puzzledly. "No, Buzz, I can't say that I have."

"Then you don't know what you're missing. It beats hell out of all the quick jumps I've ever had."

Deckard was more than halfway to his office before he realized that he'd forgotten to return Donna DuKane's apartment key.

Small wonder. The heights of nobility oft giddy the senses.

29

The office phone was ringing. Mike Madison said, "Well, Jesus Christ, I thought maybe you'd reenlisted in the fucking Marines!"

"Sometimes I stop at Vic Barsanto's. What's up?"

"Deckard, I have some things that will bring back the good old days!"

"Piss on the good old days. What are they?"

"Souvenirs from Guadalcanal. I'll bet you have a few of your own."

"Just two. A .25 caliber hole in my shoulder and a seven-inch scar."

"You didn't tell me you'd been hit. Where'd you get the scar?"

"On my ass."

"I mean *where*?"

"In Steve Javorsky's foxhole."

"Shrapnel?"

"No, I sat on Javorsky's bayonet. Thirty-some stitches worth."

"A few more like you and we'd have lost the war."

"That's what Javorsky said."

"Well, souvenirs isn't all. I have a ten-by-fifteen,

147

highly detailed scale model of Guadalcanal. I can show you the Ilu and the Tenaru and the Matanikau and Henderson Field."

"I've seen all of 'em."

"I can show you how we won that big October ruckus. You should see the tactical errors Maruyama made."

"Maruyama should see the scar on my ass."

"Can't make it, huh?"

"Not today, Mac. I'm bushed."

"Damn shame. Some other time?"

"Maybe. We'll see."

"Anything on Harry Bishop?"

"Still hacking away."

"Well, keep me up to date."

"Yeah." Deckard hung up. Madison was a warlover and his ex-mistress had been right. Guadalcanal was an obsession with him. There had been Marine Corps days that Deckard recalled with a certain amount of affection, but his stretch on Guadalcanal didn't account for any of them. Only a sick man would look back on that steamy, stinking, bleeding abcess with anything but revulsion. Deckard reached for his new quart of Sunnybrook, realizing that he'd arrived at a decision. There was no way he could conscientiously turn Donna DuKane, or Boom-Boom LaTreuse, or even Lizzie Borden, over to Mike Madison.

30

The Japanese had probed Marine positions on the night of September 12, clawing out of dense undergrowth to isolate a Marine platoon, but at dawn they'd sucked back and the Marines had buried their dead, licked their wounds, and waited. On the night of September 13 Major General Kiyotaki Kawaguchi had pulled all the plugs. Japanese infantry slammed into Marine lines at nine o'clock, at midnight, and at two in the morning. They'd come in great brown waves. Kawaguchi's eerie green flares had popped and smoked above the dripping jungle to illuminate his hordes clambering up a hundred yards of barren hillside, crouching low behind .25 caliber rifles and long, curved bayonets, frenzy boiling from their throats in hoarse shouts and screams. The Marines tore them to confetti, and still they came, scrambling up those blood-slippery, intestines-strewn slopes as Marine artillery reduced range to cut them down less than fifty yards short of hand-to-hand combat. The night had dissolved into a crimson morass of death and ear-splitting explosions, and in the sulphur-smoked canyons of Hell the Devil had cackled up a storm. The most dedicated, the most ruthless army in the history of warfare was committing suicide. Somebody had dubbed that accursed piece of ground "Bloody Ridge," but "Horror Hill" would have been far more appropriate.

Heather was shaking Deckard roughly and he was chopping his way out of it, his throat dry, the odor of death again thick in his nostrils, his body oozing cold perspiration. Heather was gasping, "Buzz! Buzz! Are you all right?"

Deckard sat up on the sweat-soaked sheet. He said, "Jesus, it was so damned *real*!"

"Have you ever had anything like this before?"

"Yeah, it happens every so often. Same old dream. Gadarukanaru."

"What? Where?"

"Guadalcanal."

"Were you there?"

"I was there. Me and General Kawaguchi and about twenty billion Japs. What the hell time is it?"

"It's after five-thirty. It's dawn, Buzz."

That was good. At dawn they always went away.

31

A note, typewritten on beige paper, had been pushed under Deckard's door: "Your immediate assistance required on matter of extreme urgency. Before noon, Room 17, Triton Motel, River Road. Don't call, come in person. I pay well." There was no signature.

Deckard took it to his desk and read it over several times. Well, it wouldn't hurt to look into it. Probably an old woman who wanted him to find her lost, strayed, or stolen toy French poodle named Jacques. Deckard had done stranger things than look for toy French poodles named Jacques, and every hundred dollars helped.

He knew the Triton Motel, a syndicate establishment. A little over a year ago he'd spent a night there with a frustrated Shakespearean actress from Spokane and in an impassioned moment she'd screamed, "Out, out, brief candle!" and it had been fully twenty minutes before Deckard regained his composure and returned to the business at hand.

He took a hefty slug from the Sunnybrook bottle and put up his Casey's Caboose sign. He drove west

151

to River Road and swung south toward Route 64. The Triton Motel was on the west side of River Road, a mile or so south of Grand Avenue, a sprawling, single-story, well-kept white-brick building set far enough back from the thoroughfare to afford a sense of privacy. He wheeled into the long, curving driveway and tooled the Olds back into the parking area. He located Room 17, pulled in next to a gleaming black Mercedes-Benz, and got out.

The door to Room 17 was partially open. Deckard knocked and said, "Hello?"

A female voice said, "Mr. Deckard?"

Deckard said, "Right."

The female voice said, "Please come in, Mr. Deckard."

Deckard stepped warily into the room, his eyes struggling to adapt from bright sunlight to the sudden dimness. The door swung shut behind him and Helen Petrakos said, "Why, Mr. Deckard, fancy meeting you here!"

Deckard mumbled something about it being a small world and stared at Helen Petrakos. She wore a pair of lace-trimmed orange panties and nothing else. Her big, hot dark-liquid eyes were glowing and at one corner of her mouth there was a slight trickle of saliva. She walked toward Deckard, her bulging bosom heaving spasmodically, her nipples flint-tipped. She pressed herself against him. There was a faint odor of spice about her. She cupped Deckard's astonished face in her hands and looked up at him beseechingly. She said, "Oh, God, please tear my panties off!"

Deckard sighed resignedly. He said, "All right, Helen." He was amazed by his own matter-of-factness.

Helen Petrakos said, "Thank Christ!" Her voice

was hoarse. She glanced down at her lace-trimmed orange panties. She said, "Rip them from my body! *Destroy* them! Then *take* me! *Abuse* me! Rape the *hell* out of me! Make me *bleed*!"

Deckard shrugged. He tossed his hat onto a chair. He slipped his fingers under the elastic band of the lace-trimmed orange panties. He looked into the turbulent dark eyes of Helen Petrakos. He said, "Now?"

"*Now!*"

"*Right* now?"

"Yes, for God's sake, *right now!*"

Deckard said, "Well, it's your motel room." He pulled with an abrupt, violent, upward, twisting motion. The lace-trimmed orange nylon clung stubbornly for a moment, then gave way without further protest to depart the olive-skinned, spice-scented body of Helen Petrakos. The crotch of the wispy garment was dripping wet.

Deckard placed his hands on her smooth, firm shoulders and he pushed, very hard. Helen Petrakos hit the middle of the bed, flat on her back, her full buttocks toward Deckard, her legs held high, her fingers clawing into the glossy black mass of hair in the middle of her. She spread herself mercilessly open and Deckard found himself staring into the eternal pink pit from which a man first plunged emerges never again the same.

Then he put on his hat and went out to his Oldsmobile, his white mantle of nobility resplendent in the noonday sun.

32

Billie Jo Spears was serving lunch at Casey's Caboose, and if the pungent odors of corned beef and cabbage hadn't spun Deckard's head, the full-blast strains of "Galway Bay" most certainly would have. Willie Clausen was at the bar, listening attentively to Casey and Deckard wondered if Casey was telling Willie about the man who'd gotten his whatsis tattooed like a yardstick. They motioned for Deckard to join the seminar, but he shook them off. At the moment sex was the very last thing he wanted to hear about.

He slid into a rear booth just vacated by an elderly couple and he watched the old folks go out. The man's hand was on her bony shoulder and her withered arm was around his waist. They were laughing at some private little joke and Deckard found himself wishing that Heather could have seen them because she was very big on that sort of thing. She called it "Love at Twilight"; one Sunday morning she'd gotten into the subject of "Love at Twilight" and Deckard had been afraid that twilight would be upon them before she finished.

Billie Jo came by with a pitcher of beer and a wet rag. Deckard said, "You want a buck for the jukebox?"

Billie Jo swished the rag across the table top. She said, "Better save it, honey. Y'all somethin' like fifteen dollahs behind."

Deckard winced. "'Galway Bay'?"

Billie Jo nodded forlornly. "Reckon so." She snapped her spearmint gum.

Deckard tried to imagine one hundred and fifty consecutive "Galway Bay"'s and his mind nearly snapped. He said, "No 'Rose of Tralee'? No some other goddam song?"

Billie Jo popped her spearmint gum and thought about it. She said, "Well, seems to me like maybe Clancy O'Day played 'When Irish Eyes are Smiling'. Y'know, Buzz, that there Irish music doan make no never-mind to me. There just ain't nuthin' like good ole country pickin' an' singin'." She departed, leaving her soggy rag to ooze milky water onto the tabletop.

Deckard pushed the rag to one side and dug for a Chesterfield. There was a strange stirring in his chest, a nameless anxiety, a feeling that a development of consequence lurked just around the bend. Deckard had experienced it before and he'd come to regard it as being remotely akin to radar. The sensation was strongly premonitional, a great deal like the one which accompanies that slow, clanking ascent to the top of the first roller coaster hill. There'd been times when it had been extremely accurate and there'd been others when it had meant nothing. The last time it had struck him with force had been more than a year ago when he'd glanced at the Arlington Park entries and noticed the name See-Gee-Zee. Instantly his radar had gone wild and

Deckard had driven directly to the track to place fifty dollars on the nose of the beast in question. See-Gee-Zee had turned out to be an aging, grossly overweight mare out for one last romp. She'd gone out winging to blaze the trail as far as the top of the stretch, but at the very first challenge See-Gee-Zee's thoughts had drifted to her cozy stall and she'd folded like a mongrel dog.

But that had been then and now it was now, and now Deckard sat in a back booth of Casey's Caboose, inhaling cabbage fumes and Chesterfield smoke, drinking beer by the pitcher, becoming slightly inebriated, then quite drunk, and getting that old radar feeling over and over again. It had nothing to do with anything in particular. There was just the *feeling*.

Shortly after ten that evening Billie Jo Spears maneuvered Deckard across West Irving Park Road. He climbed the stairs and stumbled into his office. He locked the door behind him, flopped into his swivel chair, and lowered his head to his folded forearms on the desk. He couldn't remember the last time he'd been so looped.

33

It is appointed unto man once to die, the Bible
says so. Deckard owned a Bible. He'd never opened
it, but he knew the line was in there because his
father had told him it was and his father had given
him the Bible and Deckard figured the old guy
should have known. But Deckard's father had never
made mention of the flip side. Every once in a while
it is appointed unto man to *live* and Deckard had
gotten around to living on the afternon he'd met
Heather Ralston on Belmont Avenue, near Western,
on a bridge spanning the sluggish, mucky stream
known as the north branch of the Chicago River.

The long winter had faded; the day had been
balmy in comparison to what the city had experienced since late November and Deckard was positive that he'd just seen a robin descend to the
riverbank below the bridge. Deckard was a first-
robin nut. First robins did great things for his
morale and he'd stopped his Olds beyond the west
end of the bridge and walked back to verify the
sighting. No robin. Nothing but late March debris
floating on the nearly imperceptible current of the

north branch. He'd lit a cigarette and leaned on the railing to watch the strange flotsam drift along, a patched inner tube, a legless wooden chair, a splintered drawer from an old dresser. Deckard had glanced up just in time to see Heather Ralston slip on what may have been Chicago's last patch of winter ice. She'd let out a yelp and headed directly for Deckard, waving her arms like a giant, out-of-control butterfly, and Deckard had braced himself and caught her, mainly in the interests of self-defense but also because she'd been very pretty. She'd had short, flouncy copper-gold hair, sea-green eyes, an ever-so-slightly patrician nose, and almost perfectly capped teeth. She'd worn a heavy dark-blue skirt and a navy pea coat and she'd said, "Oh, thank you, kind sir!" with a breathlessness that had been very appealing. She'd peered down at the cold, gray, filthy water and shuddered. She'd said, "There but for the grace of you go I!"

Deckard had said, "Give the credit to the man upstairs."

She'd frowned and said, "I don't believe the man upstairs would piss on the best part of me." It was a strange, bitter comment, Deckard had thought, but he hadn't questioned it. He'd merely noted that it hadn't been quite *that* narrow an escape and he'd offered to buy her a bracer. She'd demurred, but Deckard had thrown in that old line about Fate having decreed it and she'd said that it was nice to meet a fellow-believer in predestination and they'd driven to Fritzi's in Logan Square for vodka martinis. After several of those they'd had bacon, lettuce, and tomato sandwiches and they'd gone to Deckard's apartment. A couple of hours later she'd sighed and said, "Aren't I easy?" and Deckard had said, "Yes," and she'd laughed and asked how many other ex-novice nuns he'd rolled in the hay.

Sprawled naked on Deckard's bed that looked like it had been struck by lightning, Heather Ralston had talked about Heather Ralston. She was from Lebanon, Pennsylvania, and her husband had died and she'd walked the very brink of suicide before packing a few clothes and taking a bus to Harrisburg, where she'd bought an airline ticket to Chicago. After a week in the big city she'd thrown in the towel. Life was more than she could handle and she'd retreated to the church. Her six months as a postulate had gone well enough, and she'd done nearly a year as a novice before she'd realized that she'd healed, that the world was passing her by, and that she didn't want to spend the rest of her life wearing long, dark dresses in long, dark hallways on long, dark afternoons. Good weather was on the way and she'd longed for the sunshine of freedom, and that very morning she'd walked away from her solemn vows at the novitiate. She'd had no destination in mind. She'd just *walked*, and ten minutes later she'd slipped on the ice.

They'd talked until nightfall and they'd found themselves caught up in that instant rapport that comes along once in a coon's age, providing it's a very old coon. She'd told Deckard that she was penniless and she'd asked if she might spend the night and he'd suggested that she spend the next fifty years and she'd seemed favorably disposed to that.

They'd picked April Fool's Day as their anniversary and Heather had prepared a Chinese dish that the Chinese had never heard of and neither had anyone else, but it had been very tasty, and they'd gotten drunk and made love until three-thirty in the morning, a rewarding if somewhat grueling experience for a man who, at forty-seven and one-half years, operated on the theory that more than once was pushing your luck.

Deckard drifted from his memory half-dream to a sharp, pinging sound and the distinct impression that it was snowing in September on West Irving Park Road in Chicago. He switched on his desk lamp and brushed minute glass fragments from his hair and from his desktop. There was a small hole high in the window behind his chair and the slug had exited through the extreme upper left-hand corner of his east window.

Deckard killed the desk lamp and sat there in darkness, suddenly stone sober. It is appointed unto man once to die. Apparently Harry Bishop owned a Bible, too. The son of a bitch should have read the Ten Commandments.

34

It was a cool and rainy morning, an early September sneak preview of mid-November, and Deckard had one of those hangovers that lasts until noon. The matter of finding Harry Bishop was no longer a thousand-dollar money-making ruse. Now he *had* to find him. Deckard no longer enjoyed the option of blowing the whistle on Donna DuKane and walking away from it all; he'd denied himself that. Deckard just couldn't expose her to Mike Madison. He felt absolutely nothing for the woman; she was a bum, a cork on the water, and Deckard wasn't even certain that he *liked* her, but he couldn't bring himself to throw the switch. The more he saw of Mike Madison, the more he became convinced that the man was some sort of psychopath, hung up on violence and potentially dangerous to the nth degree. Donna feared Madison, obviously; otherwise, why the switch of identities from Boom-Boom LaTreuse to Donna DuKane? She was in hiding, probably for damned good reason, and Deckard knew that he hadn't heard the full story of her life with the man of the frosty-blue eyes. So, with no aces up his sleeve,

Deckard had to give Madison *some*thing for his thousand dollars and it would have to be Harry Bishop. If Madison shot Bishop's balls off, that would be plain old tough shitski because when a man starts pumping lead through your office windows, the preliminaries are over and the main event is on.

Deckard couldn't find a parking place closer than two blocks from the Greene Park Field House. He walked the distance in the gray drizzle, his hat tugged low over his eyes, head down, hands stuffed into his pockets. Just what the hell was Harry Bishop's big beef, anyway? He'd left a damned good-looking, highly passionate woman high and dry and now he was pissed off because Deckard had returned a camera and some photographs. Deckard hadn't laid a hand on her and Donna had told Bishop so. But even if they'd been wearing out a mattress, it was none of Bishop's goddam business, not any longer. If he'd wanted the woman, he should have stayed with her. But now that Wonder Woman had taken it on the duffy with some shaggy country singer here he was, back in the act, making threats and shooting holes in Deckard's windows.

Deckard wasn't an expert on firearms trajectories, but in all probability Bishop's shot had hailed from street level on the south side of West Irving Park Road. It had missed Deckard when he'd been seated and it would have missed him had he been standing. It had been high and to the right of Deckard's swivel chair. Perhaps Bishop hadn't known the office was occupied or perhaps it had been just a warning, but it had required a heaping portion of screwball fortitude to unlimber a cannon and blaze away at a main-thoroughfare second-story window at eleven o'clock in the evening. Deckard hadn't mentioned the incident to Heather because there was no telling just what sort of fatalistic soliloquy it might have triggered. Well, he'd painted himself into a nasty corner. Mike Madison wanted to kill Harry Bishop and Bishop threatened to kill Deckard, while Deckard roamed the rainy streets of Chicago with nothing to go on but a pair of vacant addresses and a couple of sexual propositions from an ex-blues singer. All this was Deckard's, plus a thoroughly bewildered woman at home, a green-eyed mystic whose fantasies would have spooked the editor of a science-fiction magazine.

Deckard cut across a muddly softball diamond, made his way around a tennis court, and was pleasantly surprised to find the Greene Park Field House door unlocked. He opened it and its hinges screeched in protest. The low concrete building was chilly, damp, and deserted save for a plump, freckled, red-headed middle-aged woman who sat at a cluttered desk paging through a paperback gothic novel entitled *The Midnight Curse of Windfall Farm*. Deckard approached the desk with extreme caution. Women who messed with that sort of reading material were borderliners and Deckard had learned to treat them with kindness and understanding, but from as great a distance as possible. He cleared his throat and said, "Beg pardon, ma'am, I'm looking for the supervisor."

The redhead chucked *The Midnight Curse of Windfall Farm* into a distant wastebasket with an accuracy born of considerable practice. She said, "You know, you gotta be crazy to read such crap."

Right away Deckard felt better.

She said, "They write that stuff for fat broads who can't get laid. Hell, I can get laid any night in the week."

Deckard said, "Uhh-h-h, about the supervisor."

"You're looking at her. The name's Rosenberry. Most folks call me Rosie." Rosie had a frank, engaging, broken-toothed smile. She accepted a Chesterfield and a light, and Deckard sat on a corner of her splintered desk to watch her blow a lopsided smoke ring. She said, "Well, at last the holocaust is behind me! Thank God, the rotten little bastards are back in school!"

Deckard laughed and regretted it. It spurred his headache to a new assault.

Rosie said, "Hey, it's no laughing matter! I've just spent two and a half months in a snake pit. This morning I'm picking up a few loose ends and then I'm gonna get crocked until the middle of June! What can I do for you?"

"I hope you can tell me how to go about getting a Greene Park Chesnuts jacket."

"The Chesnuts? That's the chess group. Chess is on the adults program and I don't handle it, but you can get a jacket by winning a chess tournament."

"That's the only way? They aren't for sale?"

"Not to my knowledge."

"Does Greene Park keep records of its chess tournaments?"

"Sure, right here." Rosie snapped a desk drawer open and dug into it.

"I hate to put you to a lot of trouble."

Rosie brushed it away. "You won't. There's been only one tournament. They held it over the Fourth of July. It caught on real good and they're planning another one for next year." She unfolded several typed sheets of paper. "Just whaja wanna know?"

"Who won the jacket?"

Rosie donned a pair of blue plastic-rimmed spectacles before riffling the pages. "Mmm-m-m, let's see, now . . . yeah, this must be him . . . he's circled in red. . . . Bishop, a man named Harry Bishop."

"Do you see a Mike Madison on that list?"

"No, but . . . well, here, maybe you'd better look for yourself."

Deckard took the proffered list and scanned it carefully. There was no Madison registered. Harry Bishop's address had been entered as South Cicero Avenue, not North Marsh Street, although he'd been living with Donna DuKane at the time of the tournament. He was leaving no trail, and with Mike Madison on the prod, Deckard couldn't flaw his judgment. He returned Rosie's list. "Much obliged. Have you met Harry Bishop?"

"I've never met any of that chess bunch. Chess players are spooks."

"Who presented the jacket to Bishop?"

"The jacket was mailed to him. They listed their sizes when they entered the tournament. Bishop's down for an XL."

All right, that put Bishop back at his South Cicero Avenue address at least twice subsequent to July 4, once to receive the new jacket and once to hang the badly abused garment in his closet. "Who did Bishop beat to win the jacket?"

Rosie said, "There's no runner-up listed."

"How many people in the tournament?"

"Damn near six hundred, if they all showed up. Sixty names per sheet, nearly ten full sheets."

Harry Bishop was the class of a field of six hundred and Mike Madison regarded Bishop as a pushover. That made Madison one helluva chess player. Rosie broke in on Deckard's thoughts. "That all?"

"Yeah, that'll do it. Thanks, Rosie."

Rosie looked Deckard over. "You're a cop, right?"

"Yeah, sort of."

"I knew it! I can spot a cop a mile away! What did this Bishop guy do wrong?"

Deckard said, "Well, for one thing, he tore a big hole in the jacket."

35

That evening Deckard walked with Heather to a neighborhood theater to see *Terror on the Thames*, a Scotland Yard flick having to do with the pursuit and eventual apprehension of a demented individual who went around sticking ice picks into young ladies, but only if they were beautiful, blonde, blue-eyed, unaccompanied and waiting for buses on Fleet Street at midnight on foggy Tuesday evenings.

Early during the film Deckard fell sound asleep in the middle of a wild chase scene, and he got to snoring, and an elderly lady seated in front of them turned around and said something about feeding time in the Brookfield Zoo lion house and Heather apologized and pulled Deckard's ear and chided him mildly and he managed to stay awake until the part where the character with the ice pick was stalking an especially lovely young thing and Big Ben was bonging out midnight and the London fog was thicker than potato soup, and then Deckard drifted off again and spilled his box of popcorn and it sounded like sixty-five tons of open-hearth slag hitting a flat tin roof and the old lady flew about three feet straight up and Heather was terribly embarrassed and the old lady packed up and lit out for the other side of the theater and the arch-fiend coldcocked a cop and escaped into the fog and Deckard went back to sleep until the houselights came up.

They walked homeward under a big butter-yellow September moon and Deckard put his hand on Heather's shoulder and Heather slipped her arm around Deckard's waist and they were very much like the elderly couple at Casey's Caboose. Deckard said, "How did the movie turn out?"

Heather said, "It was the Scotland Yard supervisor."

Deckard said, "How come?"

Heather said, "I think it had something to do with Sigmund Freud."

"But why only on Tuesday nights?"

"That was his night off."

"Sigmund Freud's?"

"No, Buzz, the Scotland Yard supervisor's."

Deckard said, "I see."

Heather said, 'Oh, I'm so glad!" She giggled and she squeezed his waist and he squeezed her shoulder, and Deckard was so much in love his shoelaces were twitching.

36

He sat in his gashed swivel chair and considered the bullet holes in his office windows, their edges sparkling jewel-like in the sunlight of September. Lately Deckard had returned to a habit acquired on Guadalcanal. He'd been glancing over his shoulder frequently, but not for Major General Kiyotaki Kawaguchi and his boys. Now he looked for Helen Petrakos and Harry Bishop. He'd have known Helen Petrakos from virtually any angle, but he wouldn't have recognized Harry Bishop if Bishop had been standing on his head and reciting the Declaration of Independence, yet Deckard looked for him anyway. He found his bottle of Sunnybrook in the bottom drawer; he wrestled briefly with the Bishop matter, and then, unaccountably, his thoughts drifted to the shady paths of long ago.

Kelly James Deckard, born in southern Illinois of poor but honest parents. Deckard smiled. Well, poor, for certain. There'd been times when their honesty had left a bit to be desired. He could recall their squirming justifications of their not always high-principled pursuit of money, the miracle lure that makes television evangelists of villains and whores of every one of us, devouring truth, conscience, and the human soul in the process. Well, honest or otherwise, he'd loved Becky and Clint Deckard and they'd loved him.

His parents had done their damndest to get rich, but it hadn't worked. Failing there, they'd been forced to try something else—living in poverty—and that had worked just dandy. Deckard could remember the rented shacks without plumbing and the pot-bellied cast-iron stoves and rooms closed off to conserve heat with the coal bin empty, the woodpile shrinking, and good weather more than two months away. He could remember fried cornmeal mush for supper when fried cornmeal mush had been all there was to *have* for supper. He remembered his mother's wardrobe of a single good dress, dark-blue in color but sweat-bleached to pale orchid under the arms. He remembered walking four miles to church twice on Sundays because there'd been no family automobile and bus fare had been out of the question.

But Deckard also remembered slow, dreamy, sun-drenched summer afternoons and star-choked evenings when his father swatted mosquitoes and strummed a cracked old guitar and sang "What a Friend We Have in Jesus" on crumbling front porches, and he remembered his mother praying aloud that her boy would never have to go away to war, but war had come and Deckard had gone away and when he'd returned he'd found their modest tombstones side by side in the little cemetery on the hill just east of town. He'd left his Purple Heart and his Bronze Star with them and he'd gone away again, this time for the last time.

It had stayed with him, the love that had moved like high-voltage current through that small family, a love that had been all around him like a swarm of benevolent honeybees, and Deckard had recognized it as love because it didn't question and he knew that healthy love never questions, that it thrives on adversity, and he supposed that this was why money mattered so little to him, his firsthand knowledge that a man can get along without it but without love he is one shot-in-the-ass son of a bitch.

Since Heather, Deckard had meandered through life as through a golden fog, barely cognizant of what went on around him. Her myriad moods mesmerized him. He'd watched her go into the kitchen to make coffee and come back an altogether different woman, and he'd loved both of her. He'd seen her go from pensive to passive to passionate more rapidly than his mind could follow, and he'd loved all three of her. Once he'd told her that he was the luckiest man alive and she'd asked why and he'd said that he had a twenty-girl harem at the cost of supporting one woman and she'd poked him in the ribs, quite hard, and deep breaths had been painful for more than a week and he'd loved her for that.

Deckard knew that he was butchering the Bishop affair, that he was no longer sharp, and that his old drive had abandoned him. He didn't give a damn. When away from Heather Ralston he thought of little but getting back to her, and when with her, he dreaded leaving her. It was all temporary, of course. No one has ever managed to throw a permanent hammerlock on pure paradise, and knowing this, Deckard concentrated on the sweet succulence of the days with her, the laughing, the reaching, the touching, the sharing, the being together.

As in all things, Kelly James Deckard lived for today and tomorrow could go scratch.

37

The phone rang and Deckard picked it up. "Galway Bay" was cascading from the receiver and Mike Madison said, "Hey, Mac, too busy to come over for a beer?"

"Never *that* busy. Crank up a pitcher."

Deckard crossed West Irving Park Road and approached the entrance to Casey's Caboose just as the door boomed open and a long-haired young fellow emerged at a high rate of speed. He was traveling headfirst and he was closely followed by a portable radio that belched rock music until it shattered against a lamppost. In the doorway stood Casey Callahan, an avenging, white-maned behemoth, teeth bared, blue eyes blazing, shaking a sledgehammer fist and bellowing a great many Gaelic unprintables. As Deckard passed him, Casey said, "That goddam cannibal music was bad enough, but I really lost my temper when the son of a bitch called Mother Machree a whore!"

Deckard made his way to the back booths and found Mike Madison holed up in one, beer foam glistening on his upper lip. Madison shoved a pitcher of beer and a glass in Deckard's direction and said, "Make yourself at home, Aristotle! What's new?"

"Somebody put a slug through my office window, that's what's new!"

"When, for Christ's sake?"

"Saturday night. Eleven o'clock or so."

"Who?"

"Had to be Bishop. Who else am I chasing?"

Madison's frosty-blue eyes boiled with excitement. "Then he knows you're on his trail!"

"Obviously."

"You've hit a nerve, Deckard! You're closer than you think!" He thought it over for a moment and shook his head. "But it just doesn't sound like Harry. Harry was a mild-mannered guy."

"So was Doctor Moriarty."

"One slug?"

"Sometimes that's all it takes."

"Now that you mention it, Harry might be a pretty fair shot. He told me he was considering joining Casimar's Pistol Club out on Mannheim Road."

"If he's a pretty fair shot, he was just throwing a scare into me."

"Why?"

"He missed."

"All right, let's go to the W's. We know who, what, when, and where. *Why*, Deckard? Where have you been lately?"

"Greene Park, but I came up empty."

"Nevertheless, you could have spooked him. Who did you talk to at Greene Park?"

"Skip it. Bishop took his shot *before* I went to Greene Park."

Madison slumped back into the booth. "So, what

the hell, it probably wasn't Harry. It was the neighborhood lush, celebrating the Labor Day weekend."

"I doubt it. How many neighborhood lushes celebrate Labor Day weekends by blowing out office windows?"

"Depends on the neighborhood, depends on the lush. Did you hear the shot?"

"No. I figure he used a silencer."

Madison rolled his frosty-blue eyes. "Oh, horseshit, Deckard! Where the hell would Harry get a silencer? That's X-9 equipment! You just don't stroll into the corner drugstore and buy a silencer!"

"You can stroll into the corner drugstore and buy a 155mm howitzer if you have the right kind of money."

"Harry didn't have that kind of green. Harry was flat-ass busted."

"Sure, he was. Harry was so flat-ass busted he bought a very fancy Buick Wildcat."

"If Harry bought a classy car, it had to be financed to the nuts!"

"Not so. Cash on the barrel-head. He bought it from a woman named Minnie Murdock in Schiller Park. Maybe he hit a hot horse."

"Harry didn't gamble."

"Did Boom-Boom have money?"

"Not a dime of her own and mighty damned little of mine. Where'd you scrounge up this information?"

Deckard said, "Not bad for a guy who sits on bayonets."

"You should follow up on this Minnie Murdock."

"That's a dead end. Her address doesn't pan out."

"Well, by God, Deckard, *I'll* look for her! I'm tired of sitting on my ass, watching O'Hara and you fall over each other! I know a few people!"

"Lots of luck. Finding Minnie Murdock won't get you Harry Bishop."

"Why not? She sold him an automobile, didn't she?"

"Yes, but the bill of sale listed Bishop's address as South Cicero Avenue."

"All right, but dammit, it's worth a shot! There might be a loose thread somewhere! Tell me about the Buick Wildcat."

"'68, gray, red pinstripes; the radio had been pulled when they found it. It's in the police pound. Bishop sideswiped a Chicago squad car and abandoned it."

"Did the cops go through it thoroughly?"

"Thoroughly enough to find a bill of sale."

Madison stood. "Somebody's missing something. I don't know what it is, but I have a hunch this Murdock broad can open some doors!"

Deckard shrugged and yawned.

Madison said, "Well, you take the high road and I'll take the low road, but I'm gonna beat you to Harry Bishop, Mac! How's this for a matchup? Cresswell's man against Red Edson's? The Gadarukanaru All-Star Game! For a pitcher of suds and a buck for the jukebox! Am I on?"

"You're on, but Bishop has a gun and he won't be a sitting duck."

"Who's looking for sitting ducks? On Guadalcanal there are six dead Japs who weren't sitting ducks!" He slammed the top of the table with the flat of his hand. He said, "Quack-quack and Semper Fidelis, you son of a bitch!" He grinned and stalked from Casey's Caboose with a purposeful stride. From the halls of Montezuma to the shores of fucking Tripoli. They say that the United States Marine Corps brings out the very best in a man. Deckard wasn't at all sure of that.

Well, the entire avenue of conversation had been kicked open by Deckard's mention of the bullet through his office windows. Telling Madison he'd been shot at might have been a mistake, but he could have done much worse. He could have told him *why*.

38

He got back to his office just in time to catch the telephone. He said, "The check's in the mail."

Heather said, "Buzzer, will you be on time this evening?"

Deckard said, "Now you know better than that."

"How late will you be? I'm fixing turkey mulligan with dumplings."

"I don't know, maybe an hour. I want to run down to the Lavender Lounge."

"On Fullerton Avenue?"

"Yeah, Fullerton and Albany. Why?"

Heather whistled. "Baby, an hour may not be enough. I've heard of that place. They say there are naughty ladies on the premises."

"You mean for money?"

"Well, honey, they just don't do it for chocolate bars these days."

"But a *cop* owns the joint."

"Oh, dear God, a naïve private detective!"

"How's *two* hours? Something just came up."

"Pack it in ice cubes and bring it home. I'm gratis."

"Not quite. How about that *Reverie* by François Carrieré?"

"Oops, that's right! Okay, let's just say inexpensive. Buzz, tonight I want to discuss a new address."

"You're moving?"

"*We're* moving."

"You're still on that kick?"

"How does Stirrup Bend, Wyoming, sound?"

"Quiet, I'd imagine."

"I've checked it out. It has a grocery store, a gas station, and a pool hall."

"No post office?"

"The mail comes over from Carbuncle Ridge. Now *there's* a *big* town."

"Probably a cesspool of iniquity."

"Well, I should say! It has *three* pool halls!"

"Wow!"

Heather said, "Certainly no place to bring up Kelly James Deckard, Junior!"

Deckard said, "Jesus, no! All that eight-ball dust!"

Heather was silent for a moment. Then she said, "Buzzer, you just don't believe that there's going to be a Kelly James Deckard, Junior, do you?"

"Nope, I know when to stop."

"You know *when* to stop, but *can* you?"

"Of course. I've just had my brakes relined."

Heather said, "We'll test 'em right after the turkey mulligan with dumplings. Hurry home!" She giggled. She said, "*Daddy.*"

Deckard smiled and returned the phone to its cradle with all the tenderness he felt for Heather Ralston.

39

Deckard sat across from Lieutenant Kevin O'Hara in a battered booth of the Lavender Lounge on Fullerton Avenue. The interior of the Lavender Lounge was a kaleidoscope of colors, none of which harmonized with anything in sight. The ceiling was royal blue and leak-splotched; the walls were gold-flecked dark-green and beer-streaked; the floor was yellow-tiled and sagging; and on the east wall, high above the booths, tiny red and orange Italian bulbs formed a pair of giant L's in script. When you got right down to it, lavender was probably the only color not in evidence.

The jukebox was silent but from the back bar a radio delivered a raspy string arrangement of "With my Eyes Wide Open I'm Dreaming." Behind the bar a scrawny, cigar-chomping bartender conversed quietly with his only customer, a chubby, cow-eyed auburn-haired girl wearing a transparent charcoal blouse, tight white slacks, and shiny black boots. She was just a youngster, twenty-one or so, but the way she'd glanced at Deckard indicated that she was one of the "naughty ladies" Heather had mentioned.

O'Hara had been drinking prior to Deckard's arrival and he was showing no signs of slowing down. He'd motioned Deckard into a booth, then grabbed a couple of glasses and a quart of Sunnybrook from the back bar, and they'd hit it off like a pair of cattle thieves. O'Hara poured more Sunnybrook and said, "This Madison is some kind of weirdo." He pulled a small leather notebook from a shirt pocket and said, "Now get this, Deckard. Madison writes under two different names, Jeremy Knight and Theodore Rooker."

Deckard said, "I knew about Knight. What did he do as Rooker?"

O'Hara checked his notebook. "*The Grim Reaper Gambit, The Fianchetto Stalemate, Murder at the Manchester Chess Club, Death Is the Checkmate*, plus a stack of short stories having to do with chess."

"He's chess-struck."

"Well, I *guess*."

"Where'd you get this stuff?"

"From my sister. She works for the main library downtown. Incidentally, she went to another *Murder Times Seven* and this time it was the mayor's own daughter who polished him off. Why the hell would a guy write under a phony name?"

Deckard said, "Well, that's not particularly uncommon. Robert L. Fish wrote under the name of Pike and Max Brand had more pseudonyms than you could shake a stick at, one of which happened to be Max Brand. It probably has to do with a change in style or subject matter. Who the hell knows? Writers are a strange bunch."

"Well, dammit, Deckard, if I ever write a book, I'm

gonna want people to know that it was me who wrote the son of a bitch!"

"Maybe Madison doesn't want publicity."

"He doesn't want publicity, but he'd going around popping off about how he's going to kill Harry Bishop. That doesn't make him a shrinking violet."

"He's close-mouthed about his writing. I've talked to him on several occasions and he's mentioned it only once."

"My sister looked him up in some encyclopedia. She says he's got to be worth a ton of money."

"Over a million, I've heard. Well, he's certainly versatile. He's gone from prizefighter to U.S. Marine to writer, and he's done well in all three fields. That calls for a whole bunch of dedication."

"It also calls for a whole bunch of insanity. You have to be three-quarters cracked to run up a score in any of those departments."

Deckard watched a long-legged, pimply-faced kid wearing a motorcyclist's cap and a purple T-shirt saunter in. He sat next to the chubby girl at the bar and the bartender moved quickly away from them to busy himself with the restacking of glasses that didn't require restacking. In a matter of moments the bar was deserted and Deckard tossed O'Hara a quizzical look.

O'Hara shrugged. He said, "I ain't joined 'em, but there's no way I can beat 'em. There's been a half dozen of 'em drifitng in and out of here for years. If one drops out of sight, another one blows in. There's nothing in it for me except maybe once in a while the trick pops for a highball."

Deckard yawned. "None of my affair."

O'Hara said, "That's the way I look at it. They don't bother anybody." He splashed Sunnybrook into their glasses and said, "I sent Shakey Lenkowski up to take another look at Harry Bishop's office this afternoon. I hope to Christ he doesn't level the whole fucking Uptown area."

"Is that likely?"

"Well, I wouldn't lay odds on it, but I wouldn't bet a dime against it. Why, just recently we went out to what was the old Club Williwaw where Madison's broad used to work. There was only one car in the whole damn parking lot and Shakey backed right into it. Now that takes talent!"

Deckard played it cool. He said, "I gather that Lenkowski's a cop."

O'Hara said, "That's strictly a matter of opinion."

Deckard said, "By the way, somebody shot a hole in my office window last Saturday night."

O'Hara grinned. He said, "Well, you can't blame Lenkowski for that. We were at target practice that night and . . ." O'Hara stopped short. He said, "Oh, my God!"

Deckard said, "No, it was Harry Bishop."

"Why Bishop? Does he know you're looking for him?"

"I guess he does. He called me and threatened to do me in." Deckard didn't get into the subject of Donna DuKane.

O'Hara's smile was sour. He said, "For a few bucks it's hardly worth it, is it?"

Deckard said, "No, but it's the only case I got."

"I like your outlook, Deckard. You'd make a real good cop."

"That might have its advantages. We'd eat regularly."

"You married?"

"Not yet. Right now my landlord thinks she's my cousin from Hubbard, Ohio." Deckard took Heather

Ralston's picture from his wallet and handed it to O'Hara.

O'Hara studied it, frowning, saying nothing. After a while he returned it and said, "Pretty little thing."

Deckard said, "Smart, too. She gets some peculiar ideas, but a man can't have everything."

"You're going to marry her?"

"She's pressing for it. She wants to get married, leave Chicago, settle down, have babies; you know how it goes."

"Yeah, I know how it goes. She's looking for the whole shot, vine-covered cottage, fireside evenings; I've heard that spiel."

Deckard shrugged. "I'm not sweating it yet. This is her most recent tangent, one of many. By the time I get home tonight it may be something altogether different, a lovers' suicide pact or finding our own tropical paradise; whatever it is, it'll have to be very romantic. She's on some kind of roller coaster and she can't get off the damn thing."

"It hasn't been so long since I went down that same old turnpike. How many times you been married, Deckard?"

"This'll make once, if it happens."

"But you're about forty-five."

"Forty-eight last month."

"Why *this* woman?"

"Because she *needs* me. I don't believe I can explain that."

O'Hara said, "We never can, Deckard. They see to it that we can't. If we could explain it, we wouldn't want it." He poured Sunnybrook. "I was married once. Damn fine woman. She worshiped the very goddam ground I walked on."

Deckard was silent. Madison had told him that O'Hara's wife had died.

O'Hara said, "I got to cocking around with a cute little hooker who was working out of here. Nothing serious at first, just another piece of ass, but she began to get to me. She was different from any woman I'd ever met. A real spellbinder. She could charm the birds right out of the trees and she convinced me that she was an angel who'd just happened to get caught between a rock and a hard place. I fell crazy in love with her. Do you know why?"

"I haven't the foggiest."

"Because she *needed* me."

Deckard nodded. "It makes a difference."

O'Hara polished off his Sunnybrook at a gulp. He said, "Deckard, good God, I went and told my wife there was another woman."

"How did she take it?"

The radio on the back bar was playing "Tango of the Roses" and there was sickness welling in the dark eyes of Lieutenant Kevin O'Hara. His voice rasped. He said, "With a full bottle of sleeping pills. I buried her last October. The next day my playmate moved on to greener pastures."

Deckard swallowed hard and said, "Oh, Christ."

O'Hara said, "Yeah, Deckard, oh, Christ."

There was the shrillness of tortured rubber ripping the Fullerton Avenue blacktop. Deckard heard a man shout an obscenity. He heard a woman scream. He watched the painted plate-glass window of the Lavender Lounge explode under the impact of a black Ford sedan driven by a man wearing horn-rimmed glasses. He had a prominent pinch-nostriled nose and a receding chin, and he battled the steering wheel with wild-eyed frenzy. After ripping out a pair of booths, the black Ford swerved to a screeching halt mere inches short of the Lavender Lounge ar. The driver lolled dazedly behind the wheel, his hat smashed down over his eyes.

Deckard looked at O'Hara. O'Hara hadn't moved a muscle. He sat in the booth, whistling tunelessly, his face devoid of expression. The scrawny bartender discarded his cigar and vaulted the bar. He waded through the debris and opened the door of the Ford. He struggled to lift the driver's hat and he finally got it done by rotating it right-to-left several times. He turned and said, "Hey, Kevin, it's Shakey Lenkowski!"

O'Hara said, "You were expecting maybe Eleanor Roosevelt?"

The bartender said, "He seems kind of all bewildered."

O'Hara yawned. He said, "Yes, I noticed that back in 1950." He struck a wooden match with his thumbnail and lit a cigarette. He refilled the glasses with Sunnybrook and they drank. He said, "Deckard, do you know how Shakey Lenkowski passed the sergeant's exam?"

Deckard lied. He said, "I haven't the foggiest."

O'Hara said, "I'll tell you sometime." He got out of the booth to accompany Deckard to the front of the building. Deckard didn't bother with the door. He stepped onto Fullerton Avenue through the broken window. O'Hara said, "Then I'll tell you how he got his driver's license."

40

It was nearly two in the morning. The pillows and blankets were on the floor, and there was silence until Heather Ralston's triumphant laugh rippled the darkness. Deckard said, "What's so goddam funny?"

Heather said, "What happened to your brakes, Buzzer?"

Deckard said, "I haven't the foggiest. I'd better get my fluid checked."

Heather said, "Oh, there was no shortage of fluid! Throw me a towel, for God's sake!" Deckard handed her a towel from the dresser drawer and she tucked it between her legs. She took Deckard's hand and held it tightly to her stomach. She said, "He's there, Buzzer, I just *know* it! Kelly James Deckard, Junior, is with me at last!" She reached to tweak Deckard's nose. "See, smarty? I told you I'd get him when I wanted him."

Deckard said, "Well, you win a few, you lose a few."

"Buzz, you didn't even *try* to stop."

"I'm well aware of that."

Heather propped herself on an elbow. She gave Deckard a very deliberate wink. She said, "How great is the fall of the mighty."

Deckard said, "This was very foolish, you know."

"Was it?"

"Certainly."

"We'll make it, Buzz."

"How?"

"It doesn't matter; just so we do it together." Deckard made no response and Heather squeezed his arm. "Are you terribly sorry?"

"I don't know. I haven't had time to think about it."

After a lengthy silence Heather said, "Buzzer?" Her voice was small in the darkened room.

Deckard said, "Yeah?"

Heather said, "Buzz, don't worry, baby, I'm on the pill."

Deckard said, "I know. Your birth-control dial is in the medicine cabinet and it's right up to date."

Heather said, "Buzz, you bastard!" She ran a hand over him. *All* over him. She said, "Oh, honey, how that's going to cost you!"

They shared a Chesterfield. Then Deckard pulled her close to him. He buried his face in her clean-smelling copper-gold hair and said, "Your turkey mulligan with dumplings was very good."

"Never mind the turkey mulligan with dumplings. How was the fucking?"

"Excellent. I love the way you twitch at the end."

"I can't keep my end from twitching." She made a purring sound and wiggled closer to him.

Deckard said, "You turn me inside out."

"That's what I'm here for, to turn you inside out."

They lay in contented silence for a time, Deckard stroking her satiny buttocks. Then he said, "Heather, do you *always* pretend?"

"What do you mean?"

"Isn't there something that's *real* to you? I mean *really* real? Something you can get your teeth into?"

"Yes, Buzzer, there's you." She bit his shoulder so hard that Deckard winced. "See?"

"Am I real to you? Are *you* real to you?"

Heather flipped over, her back to him now. She said, "Buzz, if you pretend hard enough you can make anybody real."

Deckard cupped a warm breast to knead it slowly, gently. In a while he said, "I don't believe I understand."

There was no reply. Heather Ralston was sleeping.

41

Harry Bishop's abandoned office was in the Tradesman's Building on Broadway Avenue, a block and a half south of Lawrence Avenue. Deckard found the janitor in the basement, straddling a wooden crate, draining a pint bottle of Corby's whisky. He was a good old country boy and his name was Barney Gatlin. He wore greasy blue-denim coveralls, and like the Tradesman's Building, he was ancient and teetery. They rode toward the third floor on a pitching, bucking elevator that shuddered as though it was in the advanced stages of a malaria attack. Barney Gatlin looked at the uncomfortable Deckard and grinned. He said, "Had me another cop in here late yesterday afternoon. Ole Hepzibah done scared him plumb shitless."

"Hepzibah?"

"This here ellyvator. Thass what I allus call her. Ole Hepzibah."

"Good a name as any." Deckard was gulping and clinging to the little brass triangles of the lurching cage the way a hunger-crazed jungle cat clings to the belly of a fat antelope.

Barney Gatlin said, "You ain't heard the real ridiculous part yet."

Deckard's stomach was doing somersaults. He said, "What about the real ridiculous part?"

"You wanna hear it?"

Deckard managed a ghastly smile. He said, "Yeah, I'm simply wild about real ridiculous parts."

"Well, the real ridiculous part is this here cop took the stairs when he went down."

Deckard said, "That's pretty ridiculous, all right. I've seen the stairs."

Barney Gatlin chortled. "He went express. Fell down both flights. Never stopped till he rolled into the lobby like a barrel of corn squeezin's. Sounded like Fourth of July at the Parsnip County Fair."

They went swaying past the second floor and Deckard was gritting his teeth. He said, "You're talking about a cop named Lenkowski?"

"Thass right! You know him?"

"I've heard a few stories."

Barney Gatlin opened Ole Hepzibah's rickety door and Deckard lunged eagerly from the frightening confines of the decrepit conveyance to the blessed firmness of the Tradesman's Building's third floor. Barney produced a key ring of the sort once popular with Tower of London jailers and he let Deckard into the office of the Bishop Insurance Agency. By comparison, Deckard's place on West Irving Park Road looked like the Ritz-Carlton bridal suite. One broken-down desk, one badly bent gray-metal fluorescent lamp, one straight-backed wooden chair, one rusty filing cabinet; that was the complete inventory. The drawers were empty; so was the filing cabinet, and the only item of interest was a nearly completed chess game set up on the desk. A glance told Deckard that the black was in desperate straits. If it wasn't the identical situation he'd found on the paper in Bishop's apartment, it was highly similar. Deckard said, "How long has the Bishop Insurance Agency occupied this office?"

Barney Gatlin scratched his posterior and frowned. He said, "Hell, I dunn got no idea. Ain't never been nothin' ever happened that I can hook up with. Can't recollect ever seein' nobody in here."

Deckard went to the window and looked down into Broadway Avenue. A craps game was going on across the street. An old blind negro strummed a guitar with a tin cup attached to its belly. A dark-skinned hooker stood near the curbing, twitching her broad hips and smiling fetchingly at passing motorists. A drunk came reeling north from Wilson Avenue. There'd been a time when Broadway Avenue was a clean, bustling thoroughfare. No more. Chicago's galloping destruction had overtaken it. Deckard turned away from the dismal view and handed Barney Gatlin a five-dollar bill. Barney said, "Well, thanks a heap. That there Lenkowski feller diddun gimme nothin'." They went out and Barney locked the door behind them. He said, "You want Ole Hepzibah or the stairs?"

It was a difficult decision. Deckard said, "How're you fixed for fire escapes?"

42

The September afternoon was a scorcher. The big electric sign atop the Uptown National Bank Building put the temperature at 97 degrees and the humidity was a bitch. Deckard drove west, picked up the Kennedy Expressway and headed for Mannheim Road. There'd been a recent anxiety about Heather Ralston. She'd tried to mask it with chirpy, humorous remarks, but the facade was transparent. Heather was a small-town girl with small-town sensibilities and Deckard knew that she was worried about him. He could understand her concern. The Bishop thing was coming to a head; Deckard knew that and so did Heather. It hadn't been wrapped up neatly and quickly as Deckard had predicted; it had a nasty potential and the pressure was beginning to tell on her.

Heather was right. Deckard was in a shaky racket in a rotten-to-the-core city. Deckard looked at Chicago the way you look at a drunken uncle. With affectionate disgust. For years he'd hacked out a living as a small-time snooper, underpricing the big agencies and dealing in situations that most of them wouldn't have touched with a forty-foot pole. There hadn't been a surplus of filet mignon, but it hadn't been all neckbones either. Now, if Heather was really serious about leaving Chicago, if she'd come right out and make a firm stand on the issue, Deckard knew that she'd have her way and he supposed that he'd end up in some dusty crossroads burg, frying hamburgers at the local greasy spoon or going door to door, Georgie Treacherson style, selling baby photographs. All right, so be it; it didn't matter to Deckard so long as he was with Heather. He'd turn to grave-robbing to make her happy. But Deckard wondered if there would ever be happiness for Heather. She seemed to take pleasure in uncertainty, in not knowing which way she was going; she was a gilt-edged paradox, a highly intelligent featherbrain, and Deckard was certain that her most recent tack would follow its countless predecessors into her bulging file of discarded dreams.

Meanwhile, Deckard's radar was acting up. He got off the Kennedy Expressway to take Mannheim Road south, and when he left the cloverleaf a steel-loaded flatbed semi came within a coat of paint of removing a front fender. Deckard's smile was one of relief. That must have been it. He rolled south on Mannheim, waiting for his radar to simmer down.

It didn't.

43

Casimar's Pistol Club was on the east side of
Mannheim Road at the south end of Franklin Park, a
noisy, railroad-surrounded, truck-infested little
town with the roughest streets this side of Outer
Mongolia. Casimar's was a low, flat-roofed yellow-
bricked building situated between a peep-show
establishment and an ice-cream parlor. A convenient arrangement, Deckard thought. You could get
hot pants and enjoy a pineapple sundae before
buying a six-shooter and going home to blow your
next door neighbor's fucking head off.

Deckard eased warily into Casimar's Pistol Club.
He had an abiding respect for firearms and the
inadequate people who collected them. The stac-
cato rattle of handgun fire rolled from the rear of the
building into the beige-carpeted, pecan-paneled
sales area. Deckard saw an impressive array of
sleek, polished weapons in the metal-trimmed glass
case that served as a business counter. Some were
nickled, some chromed; some had ivory grips, some
pearl; and others were plain blue steel with finely
pebbled walnut at the handles. They lay there on

blood-red velvet, gleaming softly under the bluish glow of recessed fluorescent bulbs—little killers, every one, awaiting the fond caress of a lunatic. There was enough firepower in Casimar's display case to stand off an infantry regiment for a fortnight. A large, dark-haired, doe-eyed fortyish woman came out of a room behind the counter. She wore a white dress dotted with little watermelons and her smile was warm with welcome. She said, "Good afternoon, sir!"

Deckard said, "Howdy." He looked her over. He said, "I half expected to meet a guy in a slouch hat with a big scar on his face."

She deadpanned it. "He's in a detective movie at the Rialto. I'm Sally Casimar. May I help you?"

Deckard said, "Either you have a target range or there's a whole mess of trouble in your back room."

Sally Casimar laughed liltingly. "That's the Death Angels. All ladies over seventy. The threat of rape, you know. Do you shoot, sir?"

"I kicked the habit in '42, but a friend of mine comes here and he seems to enjoy it. Harry Bishop. I suppose you know Harry."

Sally Casimar frowned uncertainly and flopped a thick loose-leaf notebook onto the countertop. She turned a few pages and ran a beautifully manicured forefinger downward along a typed column of names. "Mmmm-m-m-m, oh, yes, here he is! South Cicero Avenue?"

Deckard nodded. "When did you last see Harry?"

"I've *never* seen Harry. Apparently, he was one of Donald's customers."

"Donald?"

"My husband."

"I wonder if I might speak to Donald."

Sally shook her head. "I'm afraid not. I lost Donald in June."

"Sorry."

"Yes, it was an unfortunate thing. The Death Angels had just completed a late-evening target session. One of them left her cigarette case behind and Donald took it and ran after them into the parking lot. It was dark and I suppose they thought he was a rapist. My God, it was like the Battle of the Marne out there! Poor Donald looked like a volley-ball net!"

A sudden chill was sprinting up and down Deckard's spinal column. He lit a Chesterfield with shaking hands. He cleared his throat raspingly. He shrugged. He said, "Well, we all gotta go sometime."

Sally Casimar returned to the notebook. She looked up and said, "According to our records, Harry Bishop carries an Expert's rating."

Deckard said, "I guess that's pretty good."

Sally smiled loftily. "Experts rarely miss."

"What kind of gun does Harry rarely miss with?"

She glanced at the notebook, then pushed it to one side. She said, "One of those." She pointed with pride through the top of the glass case to an evil-looking, snub-nosed thing in the first row.

Deckard looked at it and shuddered. "What *is* it?"

"A .38 Repentino-Morté Black Mamba Mark III."

"Even the name spooks me."

"It's the leading handgun among serious marks-men. Devastatingly accurate, even at considerable distances."

"I suppose the Italians build it for the Mafia."

"The Italians don't build it. Repentino-Morté is a Japanese firm headed by one of their World War II generals."

"Kawaguchi?"

"I'm not sure. I believe he was on Guadalcanal."

"I see."

"Mr. Bishop purchased his Black Mamba here. We were offering a twenty percent markdown at that time."

Deckard said, "Well, there's just nothing like getting murdered with a cheap pistol."

Sally Casimar looked hurt. She said, "Sir, the Repentino-Morté Black Mamba Mark III is *not* a cheap firearm! It lists at four hundred ninety-nine dollars and ninety-five cents!" She managed a brand-new smile. She said, "Twenty percent off if you join our pistol club."

44

That evening, when Deckard flipped his hat to
Heather, she caught it, lost control of it, grabbed at
it, missed it, and watched it hit the floor. She kicked
it exasperatedly into Deckard's big blue armchair
and stood there glaring at it, cussing softly. Over
their martinis she was strangely subdued and Deckard said, "Okay, Heather, where's the rub?"

She was silent for a time before saying, "Buzz, just
where the hell *are* we?"

Deckard said, "In love, as I understand it."

"Beyond that, I mean."

"Heather, there's nothing beyond that. *Never*, for
anybody. What's bugging you?"

"I don't know, Buzz, not exactly. It's just that
there are times when I feel as though we're walking
a treadmill in pursuit of infinite sorrow."

"Are you unhappy?"

Heather lapsed into one of her mysterious lengthy
silences. She sat looking through the window into
gathering darkness, biting her lower lip ruminative-
ly. At last she said, "No, I don't think so . . . I don't

believe I can explain this . . . not clearly . . . not now . . ."

"Do you still want to move west?"

"No, I'm afraid that dream has taken wing."

"There's a line from a paperback gothic."

Heather's sea-green eyes were huge and penetrating. She said, "Tell me, do you believe in inevitability?"

Deckard said, "Heather, I can't even *spell* it."

"I'm talking about the hypothesis that delineates us as creatures without command of our own destinies."

Deckard said, "Look, why don't you come up with something I can understand? In the English language, if at all possible."

"Well, you see, what I'm trying to say is that perhaps whatever will be will *be*, in spite of you, in spite of me. Isn't it possible that those unseen forces, the fates that united us on a Belmont Avenue bridge, may one day see fit to sever the beauty of our relationship?"

Deckard blinked. He said, "Heather, what the hell have you been reading? Or drinking? Or smoking?"

Heather smiled. It was a sad smile, resigned, Deckard supposed, to all that inevitability she'd been talking about. Then she gasped, "Oh, *God!*" and threw herself into his arms. Her *Reverie* by François Carriéré was heady. She broke into tears. She said, "Oh, Buzzer, it's all been so terribly, wonderfully sweet!" She was breathing very heavily. Just like the broads in the gothic novels, Deckard thought.

45

It was Friday morning and Deckard's office phone was ringing. Helen Petrakos said, "Where did you disappear to the other day?"

Deckard said, "I remembered that I was overdue on a big kidnapping case."

Helen said, "You had me *crazy*! It took me the rest of the day to cool down!"

"Sorry." He wasn't sorry at all.

"I thought I'd call to tell you that I'm working on the most wonderful fantasy. Do you ever have fantasies?"

"Yes, once in a while I pretend that my car's paid for."

"I mean *sexual* fantasies. This one's *beautiful!* Wanna hear?"

Deckard jerked the Sunnybrook out of his bottom drawer and took a snort. He said, "Break it to me gently; I have a weak heart."

"Well, what happens is you make me get onto the bed on my hands and knees, stark naked. Then you remove your belt and you lash my fanny until I have this utterly blinding orgasm and I pee."

Deckard said, "On the goddam *bed*?"

Helen said, "Where else? You see I won't be able to control my bladder because the pain will be so searing I'll just come apart at the seams, sort of."

Deckard said, "Merciful Christ!"

Helen said. "I thought that might be a nice way to begin our next get-together."

Deckard said, "If that's the beginning, Good Lord, how do we *end* it?"

Helen said, "Leave it to me; I'll work it out."

Deckard said, "Well, you just better remember that the bed's all wet!"

Helen said, "What are you doing this afternoon?"

Deckard mumbled something about being tied up.

Helen squealed, "*That's* it! *Bondage!* You tie me up and beat me until I'm unconscious and when I wake up you'll be taking me in magnificent twelve-inch strokes!"

"Uhh-hh, what length strokes?"

"Twleve-inch. Won't that be wonderful?"

"Yes, wouldn't it, though?"

"Oh, my God, it'll be simply excruciating!" Her speech had grown thick with saliva.

Deckard said, "Look, Helen, I think you'd better get yourself another boy. Like maybe the Marquis de Sade. He'd give you a run for your money."

"Is he in the book?"

"He's in several." Deckard hung up, locked his office, and crossed West Irving Park Road to Casey's Caboose. He found an unoccupied booth, ordered a pitcher of beer, gave Billie Jo a dollar for the jukebox, and settled into his thoughts.

He was disturbed. Heather was acting more strangely than usual, a difficult feat, even for Heather; Helen Petrakos was rapidly developing into a first-class menace; and he knew that somewhere along the line he'd managed to miss an important factor in the matter of Harry Bishop, a loose end that he should have grabbed much earlier in the ball game. He was hung up in a mess, the likes of which he'd never seen. The man who'd hired Buzz Deckard wanted to murder the man who was threatening to murder the man who was trying to protect him from the man who'd hired Buzz Deckard. Gilbert and Sullivan, where, oh where, can you be? Deckard was beached.

He swilled beer until five in the afternoon, kicking the shapeless affair around in his mind. At last he left the booth and called O'Hara at the Lavender Lounge. O'Hara said, "What's happening, Brizzolara?"

"This is Deckard. Nothing's happening. What's with you?"

"Not much. That Buick Wildcat of Bishop's was smoking. Stolen in Cleveland. Now we're looking for Bishop *and* Minnie Murdock. That's all I have."

Deckard returned to his booth and sat down with an audible sigh. He had nowhere to go and nothing to do when he got there. Time was running short; his radar told him so. Madison would catch up with Bishop or Bishop would catch up with Deckard. Deckard had to pull a rabbit out of his hat. Where the hell was the loose end? Donna DuKane? Not likely. She worked in the Loop, she'd told him, one night a week, Fridays, and this was a Friday. When he'd asked her what sort of work she did, she'd said something about it consisting of hoping for broader and brighter horizons. Hardly a definitive response. It had been just vague enough to prick Deckard's curiosity. She'd said that she left the apartment at six o'clock on working nights. Deckard glanced at his watch. Nearly five-thirty now. Well, what the

ROSS H. SPENCER

hell, nothing ventured, nothing gained. He lef
Casey's Caboose, piled into his Oldsmobile, anc
drove west to North Marsh Street. He parked a fev
doors up the street from Donna's building and sa
there in the hazy afternoon, sweating, smoking, anc
listening to the late afternoon news. The Cubbie:
were in a state of utter disarray and rapidly drop
ping out of the pennant chase. That was bad. Ho Ch
Minh was dead. That was good.

At five minutes before six a bronze Jaguar pullec
up in front of the old brown-shingled two-flat. It wa:
driven by a silver-haired man who tooted the horn
leaned back, and lit a cigar. In a couple of minute:
Donna DuKane came down the back steps and uj
the walk, carrying a small overnight bag. She tucke
herself into the Jaguar and it zipped away from the
curb, headed south. Deckard tagged it all the way to
the Loop, running three stoplights over the dis
tance. When the expensive British car whiskec
abruptly into the Monroe Street parking lot, Deck
ard followed it in warily, his hat tilted forward to
shield the upper part of his face. A diminutive
bespectacled attendant, clad in red-trimmed white
coveralls and a gold-braided blue cap, dashed self
importantly in a great many directions to contro
traffic, waving his arms frenziedly, like he wa
conducting the Philadelphia Philharmonic in the
grand finale of *The Firebird Suite*. He hustled the
Jaguar into a parking stall on the right and h
motioned Deckard into one on the left, a bit furthe
to the north.

Deckard kept his head down, watching the littl
guy open the door of the Jaguar for Donna DuKan
and then scurry squirrel-like around the car t
accept a tip from the silver-haired driver. Whe
Donna and her escort left the parking lot, Deckar

210

scrambled hurriedly out of the Oldsmobile to pick up their trail. Another wild-goose chase, beyond doubt, but Deckard had been pursuing wild geese since he'd been old enough to remember. He found his route blocked by the parking lot attendant who stood, hands on hips, shaking his head disapprovingly. He said, "Not *that* stall! The *next* stall!"

Deckard said, "But *this* is the stall you pointed to."

The attendant said, "No, I pointed to the *next* stall."

"Well, what the hell's the difference? The lot's three-quarters empty!"

"That stall's reserved. It belongs to J.B. Mahoney."

"Screw J.B. Mahoney! I'm in a hurry!"

"Sure, you are, just as soon as you move that automobile to the next stall." He was a defiant little gamecock.

Deckard tossed his keys to the attendant. He said, "*You* move it. It's worth a sawbuck when I get back."

The attendant threw the keys back to Deckard. He said, "I *can't* move it."

Deckard said, "Well, why the hell not? For a sawbuck I'll move the frigging *Queen Mary!*"

"I don't know how to drive, that's why not. Now do you move that car or do I call a cop?"

Donna DuKane and her silver-haired companion were no longer in sight and Deckard sagged against a fender of the Olds. He said, "This must be some kind of fucking nightmare."

"Come on, buddy! J.B. Mahoney will be pulling in here any damn minute now!"

Deckard shrugged and got back into the Oldsmobile. He said, "By the way, what's your name?"

The attendant bristled. He said, "Bonaparte! What about it?"

Deckard said, "Jeez, what a coincidence! Mine's Wellington. *Duke* Wellington."

He drove directly to Casey's Caboose, grabbed a bottle of Old Washensachs and the telephone. He called O'Hara. He said, "O'Hara, can you get me a fast make on a license number?"

O'Hara said, "Why?"

Deckard said, "I haven't the foggiest. The plates are on a bronze Jag." Deckard gave him the license number and the number of the phone at Casey's Caboose.

O'Hara said, "Gotcha. Is this important?"

"I doubt it."

"I'll get back to you."

Deckard waited by the phone. O'Hara called back and said, "Byron Drake, 326 West Alles in Des Plaines. Does that help?"

"Not a bit."

A frown crept into O'Hara's voice. He said, "Well, Jesus H. Christ, Brizzolara, you could have run it down yourself. What the hell, you're a cop."

"This isn't Brizzolara; it's Deckard."

"Well, you sound just like Brizzolara on the phone."

"Who's Brizzolara?"

"A cop I'm supposed to have coffee with one of these mornings."

"Pete Brizzolara?"

"Yeah, you know Pete Brizzolara?"

"I wouldn't know Pete Brizzolara from Robin Hood."

O'Hara said, "Well, Deckard, the way you can tell the difference is Pete Brizzolara don't got no fucking bow and arrow."

Deckard hung up and headed for the bar, frowning. Willie Clausen said, "Hey, Buzz, did you hear about that new X-rated joint out at Mannheim and Fullerton?"

Deckard shook his head.

Willie said, "Man, we just gotta get out there some night! They got a broad who does it with a reindeer!"

Deckard said, "Does Santa Claus know about this?"

Willie said, "There ain't no Santa Claus."

Deckard said, "Who told you there ain't no Santa Claus?"

Willie said, "The Tooth Fairy."

Deckard drank ten bottles of beer and went home half-barreled. Sometimes that's all there is to do in Chicago.

46

Deckard didn't reach his office until eleven the next morning. Heather had been deep in the dark-blue doldrums. He was familiar with many of her moods, but this was no three-for-a-dime state of depression. She'd sat on the couch, her legs tucked under her, sipping glass after glass of cranberry juice, chain-smoking, gnawing on her lower lip, staring through the window, saying absolutely nothing. He'd tried a dozen approaches, but he'd been unable to pierce her new armor; so he'd put on his hat and checked out.

He opened his office door to find a slip of paper on the floor, a curt, typed note advising him that there was no Marquis de Sade in the telephone book and further advising him that his rent would be $400.00 per month, effective October 1. Hell hath no fury like a Greek landlady spurned.

Deckard opened his bottom desk drawer and took out Galahad IV and his bottle of Sunnybrook. He dug Harry Bishop's wrinkled chess problem out of the Old Washensachs can and he smoothed it on the surface of the desk, once again arranging the pieces to comply with the drawing.

The black didn't have a prayer, not one chance in a zillion, but the problem specified that the white win in three moves, and no matter how one-sided the situation, winning in a particular number of moves is often easier said than done. Deckard shoved Helen Petrakos out of his thoughts, deposited Heather Ralston lovingly on an unlighted back burner, took a nip from the Sunnybrook bottle, lit a Chesterfield, and hunched forward, elbows on his desk, chin cupped in his hands. All right, now was the hour. He was about to take his first real shot at the Bishop problem.

The hell he was.

Mike Madison came into his office, quietly this time, without his usual bull-of-the-woods swagger. He sat on a corner of Deckard's desk and said, "Mac, I'm going to need you tonight."

Deckard said, "Not tonight. I have difficulties at home."

"It's important. Deckard, I've located that woman." There was sober, quiet urgency in his voice.

Deckard said, "Well, that's just ginger-peachy. *What* woman?"

"The one who sold Bishop the Buick Wildcat. Minnie Murdock."

Deckard said, "I talked to O'Hara yesterday. That car was stolen in Cleveland."

"Harry got skinned?"

"I don't know the ins and outs of it, but the car's hot. Where's Minnie Murdock?"

"On 73rd Court in Elmwood Park."

"How did you locate her?"

"It cost me. I wangled her forwarding address out of a guy at the Schiller Park Post Office. Her new phone's unlisted, but a connection at Illinois Bell dug up the number."

"So what good is she?"

"What *good* is she? Deckard, she has Harry's new address!"

Deckard felt a tingle romp across the back of his neck. He said, "Oh, boy!" His radar had been right and the fur was about to fly!

Madison said, "Harry used his South Cicero Avenue address on the bill of sale, but he told Minnie Murdock that he'd be moving shortly. The Buick's radio was in a repair shop. Minnie's son was supposed to pick it up and bring it to Bishop's new apartment. That's how she got the address. Harry scribbled it on a match-flap."

"So where's he holed up?"

"There's our final hurdle. She has the address, but all she can make of it is that Harry's somewhere in River Grove. Harry has an atrocious handwriting."

"You couldn't figure it out?"

"I haven't seen it. I talked to Minnie Murdock on the phone. She isn't particularly anxious to see Harry again. The repair shop folded and she can't get the radio back."

Deckard said, "All right, let me handle it. I'll go

see her and I'll decipher it. I know River Grove like the back of my hand."

"That's been arranged. She'll bring the match-flap to your apartment about ten this evening."

"Why my place? Why so late? Heather's off her feed as it *is*."

"I know it's an inconvenience, but Minnie will be visiting her daughter over on Terrace Place, a block and a half from you. Birthday party on her grand daughter."

"What a downright sweet old broad. She peddles hot cars and then toddles off to a birthday party on her granddaughter."

"She says she bought the car at an auction. Maybe she did, who knows? Anyway, she'll walk over to your apartment with the match-flap and you'll give her this." Madison folded a one-hundred-dollar bill and handed it to Deckard. He said, "Give the old ba a lift home."

"And then comes the big Dodge City shoot-out?"

Madison said, "No, Mac, no shoot-out. Call me and give me the address and I'll relay it to Lieuten ant O'Hara. Let me have the pleasure of blowing the whistle on Bishop and putting the needle to O'Hara then I'm through with the whole rotten can o worms. I've had it!"

Deckard leaned back in his swivel chair, his jaw sagging. He said, "Well, I'll be dipped in moose manure!"

Madison said, "I've done some serious thinking. have you to thank for that, Deckard, and I'm thank ing you, here and now! I'm lucky I came to you instead of some bastard who doesn't give a damn You pumped some sense into my head. I can't pla by Guadalcanal rules. What the hell, I'm over fift and I'm sitting on top of the world; why should I ris everything by killing a shitheel like Harry Bishop? He isn't worth it and neither is Boom-Boom. Even if I got away with it, she'd fly the coop again." Tears glistened in Mike Madison's frosty-blue eyes. The man of granite was a marshmallow and Deckard's heart rushed out to him. Madison said, "Deckard, piss on the sexy young floozies! What I need is a big fat mama my own age, one who'll cook sauerkraut and thuringers and bake applesauce cake and tuck me into bed at night."

Deckard studied Madison, liking what he saw. Here was a weary old war horse, yearning for green pastures and a cold, clear brook. Deckard said, "Mac, I hope to God you find your big fat mama." He meant it. He shoved out his hand and Madison took it, bearing down on it like a five-hundred-dollar vise. Deckard said, "I'm not sure you got your money's worth."

Madison gave Deckard a deprecatory wave of a big, horny hand. "Knock off that crap! You've been worth every damned dime, you busted-down old gyrene! You've been an utter delight! Buy your girlfriend a jug of perfume."

Deckard said, "A thousand dollars will buy a tank car of perfume."

Madison squinted at him. "Depends on the perfume, Mac. François Carrieré puts out something called *Reverie* that goes for about two hundred an ounce." He popped from the corner of the desk, upsetting a few of Galahad IV's chess pieces in the doing. He returned them carefully to the playing board and dug into a shirt pocket for a slip of paper. He said, "Yeah, while I'm thinking of it, here's the solution to that damned nickel-and-dime chess problem. I'm surprised you haven't tumbled to it by now."

Deckard took the paper and dropped it onto his

desk. He left his swivel chair to see Madison to the
door. He said, "I'll call you when I've driven Minnie
Murdock home."

"Do that, Mac! They'll bust Harry's ass for hitting
that squad car. I could visit him in the lockup and
pee on him through the bars." He shuffled self-
consciously for a moment before saying, "Well, hell,
Deckard, maybe it wasn't a total loss. I think I can
get a book out of it. You know the bit—aging man
finds himself at last, that sort of rot."

"Autograph a copy for me."

"Right! 'To the guy who sits on bayonets.' Okay,
Mac?"

Deckard grinned. "Okay, Mac!"

Madison waved and went out and Deckard returned to his swivel chair, feeling like an anvil had
been lifted from his chest. He picked up the telephone to agitate Heather about François Carriere's
"cheap" perfume. When there was no answer, Deckard glanced at the clock and smiled. Nearly noon.
Heather would be across the street again, reading
the riot act to Fanny Duncan about her dog. Hooray
for the Duncan dog! Tonight things would return to
normal in the Deckard domicile.

47

How had Charles Darwin described curiosity?
. . . damnable? . . . detestable? On West Monroe
Street Deckard's grin was shamefaced. Darwin was
probably right. He swung the Olds into the Monroe
Street parking lot. Bonaparte pointed to a parking
stall and glared as Deckard drove by. He yelled,
"Hey, Wellington, try to get it right this time!" Well,
that was a step in the right direction. Bonaparte had
a memory for automobiles, faces, and names. Deckard pulled into the designated stall and leaned back
to wait. Eventually Bonaparte arrived at the Olds,
mopping his brow with a coveralls sleeve. He said,
"You did better this time. You can go now."

Deckard said, "Look, Bonaparte, remember that
bronze Jaguar that got in here just ahead of me early
yesterday evening?"

"Sure, with the cute blonde quiff and the guy that
got the rebel drawl. Man, Wellington, I like the way
that broad walks!"

"So do I. Who are those people?"

Bonaparte winked at Deckard. He said, "What's
the difference? You a private detective?"

221

Deckard winked back. "That's the difference."

Bonaparte dashed away to usher a gray Dodge into a parking slot. When he returned he said, "That ain't a big enough difference."

Deckard said, "Twenty bucks says you don't know 'em."

"Of course I know 'em! I been parkin' 'em every goddam Friday night since spring. You tailin' 'em?" Bonaparte left to handle a dark-blue Rolls-Royce. He came back, tucking a five-dollar bill into his coveralls pocket. "That was J.B. Mahoney. J.B. Mahoney shaves with a chainsaw. *Terrible* temper!"

Deckard said, "Let's forget about J.B. Mahoney. Tell me about the people in the Jaguar. Who are they and where do they go on Friday nights?"

Bonaparte shook his head and grinned foxily. "Not for twenty, Wellington. How's fifty?" He ran to make wild signals to an approaching Ford LTD, simultaneously motioning for Deckard to pull up beside him. When the LTD had been disposed of, Bonaparte leaned into Deckard's Olds and took the fifty dollars. He said, "The guy's name is Drake. I'm not sure about the blonde chick but Drake always calls her Dee-Dee."

Deckard nodded. D.D., probably, for Donna Du-Kane. "Okay, what's the rest of it? Where do they go?"

"They're actors. They're in that *Murder Times Seven* play over at the Ghent-Rumley on East Adams Street."

48

Donna DuKane made no immediate response to
Deckard's tapping on the window of her kitchen
door. Deckard rapped once more and waited in the
golden late-afternoon, a foot up on the second-floor
back-porch railing, conscientiously free of the Harry
Bishop tangle at last. He was out of it and he was out
of it for keeps. Madison hadn't leveled with him.
Madison's prodigal shack-job was a member of the
Friday evening *Murder Times Seven* cast and that
photograph of the pair had been snapped at some
sort of theatrical doings, probably a curtain call or a
post-performance cocktail party. Madison had
known where she was all along, and he'd known
Bishop's whereabouts until Bishop had left 4222
North Marsh Street in late August. All that talk
about looking for Bishop since spring had been so
much hogwash. Madison had probably been dicker-
ing with Donna DuKane ever since she'd fled Timberwood Estates, but she'd refused to renew the
alliance. Her answer had doubtless remained the
same after Bishop had dropped her, leaving Madison
one possible balm for his badly bruised ego—kill the

sonofabitch who'd been responsible for the break. If he'd gone after Bishop while Bishop was living with her, Donna would have talked to the police, but now she might not even hear of Bishop's demise and there was little chance that she'd fret over it if she did. Now Madison's route was clear, but his quarry had disappeared. However, when Madison was in possession of Bishop's new address, the jig would be up. Madison had no intentions of contacting Kevin O'Hara. He'd blow Bishop away unceremoniously and Deckard would have gained the dubious distinction of being the finger-man. Well, if Madison was going to get to Harry Bishop, it wouldn't be with Deckard's assistance. Tonight, when Minnie Murdock handed over Bishop's match-flap, Deckard was going to flush it down the toilet without so much as looking at it. Then he'd call Mike Madison and tell him exactly where he could shove the whole fucked-up affair.

The picture was a fuzzy tangle and Deckard was having trouble getting it straight in his mind, but he was dead certain of one thing—he was hosting the 1969 Screwball Convention. Harry Bishop stole a woman, junked her, tried to come back to her, and issued death threats to her visitors when he couldn't swing it. According to no less an authority than Mike Madison himself, Donna DuKane, or Boom Boom LaTreuse, spent most of her time on cloud #44. Helen Petrakos was a sex maniac capable of routing a regiment of veteran satyrs; Madison was carrying on in a fashion befitting a fugitive from Bedlam; and Heather Ralston's inexplicable dark moods were occurring with alarmingly increasing frequency. Yea, verily, the inmates were seizing control of the cracker factory.

Well, he was about to confront Donna DuKane

previously known as Boom-Boom LaTreuse. He'd make his explanations, if she'd accept them, and he'd hear hers, if she had any to offer. Then he'd pick up his marbles and go home. This time next month he'd be with Heather in a cozy Pennsylvania Dutch restaurant near Lebanon, drinking dark beer and working on an order of sauerbraten. This weird little circus was all but behind him.

Deckard lit a cigarette and looked out over the clean, sun-splashed neighborhood, watching a pair of blond tykes cavorting in a red plastic wading pool, a tousel-headed teenage kid removing the front wheel of an old blue bicycle, a heavyset woman with her stringy dark hair done up in a tight bun, lugging the day's garbage out to the alley. The view was serene and Deckard turned his back on it with reluctance. He knocked once more, and when there was no answer, he found Donna DuKane's key and let himself in. If she wasn't at home, he'd leave the key and a bye-bye note.

The apartment was stuffy, dim, and quiet. Deckard said, "Anybody home?" The silence was heavy. *Too* heavy, it occurred to Deckard. He started toward the living room, then froze in his tracks like an old hunting hound. There's an odor that a man never forgets and Deckard had made its acquaintance on Guadalcanal. Suddenly he found himself wishing to Christ that he'd brought the gun he never bothered to carry.

From the kitchen he could see that the living room was unoccupied. He stepped around his better judgment and looked into the bathroom. Nothing of interest. He turned the corner into the bedroom and recoiled, his knees nearly buckling under him.

Donna DuKane had made her final curtain call and Boom-Boom LaTreuse had sung "Fascination" for the last time. She stared at him from the bed they'd never shared, her brown eyes wide and bulging, her mouth agape, the lips drawn tightly back against her white, even teeth in a ghastly smile of stark horror. She lay naked on her back, her long tawny legs spread wide, drawn up at the knees, and between them, on her and *in* her to the hilt, sprawled her companion of the previous evening, his silver head nestled in the gentle curve of her shoulder.

The bed was a splattered surrealistic nightmare in blood, and blood had trickled between them, a crimson mucilage gluing their bodies together. They'd been dead for some time—twelve hours or longer was Deckard's educated guess—Byron Drake shot through the side of his head, Donna DuKane an inch or so above her left eyebrow; both at extremely close range. It hadn't been the work of an overwrought killer, the kind that starts shooting and pulls the trigger until the clip is exhausted. Harry Bishop had been coolly professional. He'd lurked in the bedroom closet until the festivities had gotten under way; that was obvious. The closet door was ajar and ladies awaiting lovers don't leave closet doors open.

In her closing split seconds of existence Donna DuKane had witnessed the approach of death, but Byron Drake had been blissfully oblivious to it. Bishop had struck quickly and with Mafia-style efficiency. He'd killed the right woman, but he'd never seen Deckard and he'd shot the wrong man. There, but for Deckard's new-found nobility and the ever-loving grace of the crucified Jesus Christ, lay the rigid body of Kelly James Deckard. And aside from Mike Madison, Kelly James Deckard was the only son of a bitch on earth who could possibly link

Harry Bishop with Donna DuKane. It would be only a brief matter of time until Bishop learned of his error, and then look out!

Deckard backed slowly from the grisly sight on the bed, and on his knees in Donna DuKane's pink-tiled bathroom, he became quite sick to his stomach, the horror flashing before him with his every purging convulsion. He found himself marveling at the irony of Almighty God's greatest jest. Why must a man's finest erection come after death?

49

Deckard climbed the stairs on numb legs, slammed his office door behind him, and threw the security bolt. He took his .45 Colt automatic from the filing cabinet, released the safety, and placed the weapon in his top desk drawer, leaving the drawer slightly open. He pulled his office blinds, flopped limply into his swivel chair, and drank deeply from his bottle of Sunnybrook. He lit a cigarette and noticed that his hands were steadying just a bit. He sat there with twilight beginning to close in, his thinking apparatus clanking as discordantly as his antique air conditioner, going back to 4222 North Marsh Street and a dead man mounted up on a dead woman. Necrophilia in spades. The brazen jangle of a bell ripped a gaping hole in his fog and through it Deckard reached for the telephone. He said, "The check's in the mail."

The voice said, "This is E. Plúribus Unumberto. Deckard? Kelly J. Deckard?"

"Yeah."

E. Pluribus Unumberto said, "You know me, Deckard. I'm the barkeep out here at Jake's Joint on

Milwaukee Avenue. Where the old Club Williwaw was."

"Yeah."

"You were here the other day, right after that bonehead cop smashed up my automobile. Remember?"

"Yeah."

"Well, I got a hot item on that Boom-Boom La-Treuse broad you were asking about."

"Yeah?"

"Hey, Deckard, that's sure a fancy vocabulary you've put together!"

"Sorry, Unumberto, what did you turn up?"

"Well, one of my old customers just ran into Boom-Boom LaTreuse!"

"When?"

"This very afternoon, for Christ's sake! She was hanging around the Green Mill Tavern on Armitage Avenue, only she wasn't Boom-Boom LaTreuse and she wasn't singing no blues!"

"Go on."

"She was Corkie Henderson and she was selling her ass at twenty-five bucks a copy!"

"That's impossible."

"The hell it's impossible! This is the *second* time he's seen her!"

"When was the first time?"

"About a year ago, he said, but a year ago she was Holly Webster and she was working out of the Lavender Lounge on Fullerton. He told me that he even bought her a drink and they were talking about Dorothy Neff."

"Who's Dorothy Neff?"

"I told you about Dorothy Neff. She was the loon who rode bare-ass on the hood of some drunk's car and wiped out an army convoy."

"Oh, yeah. Whatever became of Dorothy?"

"Well, Boom-Boom or Holly or Corkie or who-the-ell-ever was telling this guy that Dorothy picked up a job as a wing-walker with Captain Billy Armstrong's Air Carnival."

"Nude?" Deckard's voice was flat, dull.

"Not this time. They made her wear goggles."

"Well, thanks anyway, Unumberto, but your cusomer has his women scrambled. I've located Boom-Boom LaTreuse. She died very recently."

"I'm a dirty son of a bitch! You *positive* of that?"

"Sure am. I saw her body."

"Damn! Well, Deckard, I'm sorry to hear that. Didn't mean to take up your time."

"No problem. I appreciate your interest."

"Did you ever get to hear her sing?"

Deckard said, "No, I came in a little late for the music."

50

Darkness threw a shroud over the sick gray city on the shores of polluted Lake Michigan, and Deckard sat in his office, pulling at his bottle of Sunnybrook and thinking about E.P. Unumberto's call. Odd that an old Williwaw customer could be wrong *twice* after so short a period of time. How long had it been since the Williwaw had been a flourishing tits-and-ass establishment? Two years, three? Probably four at most, although he wasn't really up on the history of the place. Still, as Unumberto had told him at Jake's Joint, there'd been a deluge of girls and none of them had hung around long enough to become well acquainted with the regular bartender, let alone with a nut who dropped in on spaced-out occasions to ogle the merchandise. Unless she was a real stick-out, remembering one girl of the Williwaw smorgasbord would be a bit difficult. On the other hand, Boom-Boom LaTreuse had been just the sort of female a man might recall, because E.P. Unumberto had returned her to mind with a modicum of difficulty. Deckard took his lop-eared telephone book from a corner of the desk and paged through it. He called the Green Mill Tavern or Armitage Avenue and said, "I'd like to speak to Corkie, please."

"Corkie who?" The voice was masculine and surly.

"Corkie Henderson. How many Corkies you got?"

"Corkie's out at the moment. Care to leave a message?"

"Not really. When will she be back?"

"Maybe an hour. What's on your mind?"

"I was thinking about getting together with her. I was in there a week ago and we were talking."

"Come off it, buddy! Corkie just started this afternoon!"

Deckard hung up. If he hadn't been downright terrified, he'd have considered driving to the Green Mill before going home. He wondered if Heather would be able to read him and know that he'd been badly shaken. Probably. Heather was observant. He continued his Sunnybrook attack, letting its glow disperse his lingering chill, mulling the suddenly murderous situation over and over, and staring almost without thought at Harry Bishop's chess problem on his desk. *Almost* without thought, but not *entirely* without thought. Deckard frowned. There was something *different* about that problem, a change since he'd looked at it prior to Mike Madison's visit earlier in the day.

Deckard glanced at the paper he'd found in Harry Bishop's jacket pocket. He picked up the solution provided by Madison and he studied it. He looked at the chess board again. His ears were beginning to ring the same way they'd clanged under the influence of malaria-healing quinine on Guadalcanal twenty-seven years ago. Cold beads of sweat were beginning to form on his forehead and the hair on the back of his neck was prickling. The room was turning, slowly at first but with ever-increasing speed. Deckard battled his way from the vortex of the thing and lunged for his telephone.

It was time to call up the heavy artillery.

51

Lieutenant Kevin O'Hara came clomping up the stairs at 8:25 that evening and Deckard threw the security bolt to let him in. The burly Irish detective was sweating like a mule skinner. As Deckard returned to his swivel chair, O'Hara plucked the bottle of Sunnybrook from the desk and took a lusty belt. He fixed Deckard with an unsympathetic eye. He said, "Deckard, I had to leave Shakey Lenkowski in charge of my tavern, so this better be mighty goddam good."

Deckard said, "O'Hara, have you ever played chess?"

"Played hell out of it in the army and haven't messed with it since. Jesus Christ, you didn't bring me clear the hell up here just to ask me if I ever played chess, did you?" He glared at the chess problem on Deckard's desk.

"Ever solve any chess problems?"

"Fooled around with them occasionally. I never was a whiz at figuring them out. Get to it, Deckard; by now the Lavender may be going up in flames."

Deckard said, "You're looking at a chess problem

I found in a jacket pocket in Harry Bishop's apartment on South Cicero Avenue. It calls for the white to move and mate in three moves."

O'Hara glanced briefly at the arrangement on the chess board. He scowled and said, "*Three* moves? Why not *one*?"

"Because the problem specifies *three*. Madison dropped in on me today and he gave me the solution to that problem." Deckard passed Madison's slip of paper to O'Hara. He said, "Tell me what's wrong with this."

O'Hara's dark, intelligent eyes flicked from the paper to the chess board to the paper to the chess board to the paper, like those of a man watching a rapid game of table tennis. He shook his head and said, "This solution says that on the first move the White Knight places the Black King in check by capturing a Bishop on Black King's Bishop's Second."

Deckard nodded. "That's what it says. With that White Knight on Black King Bishop's Second, the Black King's compelled to move to the Knight's First; he has no other choice. Then the same White Knight captures a pawn and the Black King's right back in check, so he returns to his Rook's First; again no choice. That's when the very same White Knight captures the Black Queen and you have a 'discovered' checkmate with the unmasked White Rook providing the coup de grâce."

O'Hara said, "Sure, Deckard, that's what this *solution* says, but the fucking *chess board* says it's a *one*-move checkmate, White Queen to Black King Knight's First!"

Deckard said, "Right! So how does the chess board disagree with Madison's solution?"

"It disagrees on the first goddam move. The White Knight *can't* capture a bishop."

"Why not?"

"Because there *is* no Bishop."

Deckard shrugged. He took a very stiff slug of Sunnybrook and passed the bottle to O'Hara. He said, "That's right, O'Hara. There *is* no Bishop."

O'Hara dropped heavily onto the client's chair. He sat in silence for the better part of a minute. Then, ever so slowly, he raised the bottle to Deckard and his smile was a smile from the battlefield at Clontarf. He said, "I'll drink to that."

52

It was nine-forty, too early for Minnie Murdock to arrive with Harry Bishop's match-flap, but it wasn't too early for Deckard's memories. Here they came, those carefree golden ghosts, writhing out of the recent past to romp through his living room, grimacing, leaping, laughing. There'd been the afternoon at Wrigley Field when Heather had gotten sunburned because she was fair-skinned and Deckard hadn't because he wasn't and they'd gorged themselves on hot dogs and cold beer and the Cubbies had won it in the thirteenth with an awesome display of power—a hit batsman, an infield error, a balk, and a wild pitch. There'd been the time when he'd tried to teach her to shoot pool and she hadn't pocketed a ball and Deckard had made all seven of his, but he'd scratched when he'd sunk the eight ball and that had made Heather the winner and she'd never let him hear the last of it. There'd been her weekly put-on, singing "Fascination" in that sweetly husky voice, making big goo-goo eyes at him and stroking his face until she cracked up with laughter. Deckard brushed a sudden tear from his cheek, the first time he'd done so since he'd stood at his parents' graves in 1945.

A couple of kids sauntered past his garden apartment window, a boy and a girl, both fifteen or so, using language that would have curdled the blood of a New York City longshoreman. A diesel locomotive horn bellowed from the CMStP&P railroad crossing in Elmwood Park. Across the street the Duncan dog howled dismally. Then the living room grew still as a tomb and the minutes grated along on little leaden feet.

A man passed the window, a tall fellow, very much in a hurry, whistling "Colonel Bogey" in cadence to the briskness of his stride. Then, again, silence, an avalanche of it, the silence of fear. Deckard had known pockets of such silence on Guadalcanal, waiting for the green flares of midnight and the banzais and the unearthly screech of Japanese tin bugles and the hell of explosions and the awful screams of the dying, and at this moment, Deckard felt no safer in Chicago than he had on Guadalcanal.

Nothing for several minutes, nothing at all, and then faint footsteps from the south, footsteps growing closer; slow, heavy footsteps, unrhythmic and rasping on the sidewalk of Miriam Avenue. A sturdily built elderly woman hove into view, her frowsy hair a gray beacon in the glow of the streetlight, lurching along, carrying a paper shopping bag. She paused at the short walk leading to Deckard's apartment steps and in a moment she was descending those steps, her shopping bag clattering against the rough brick surface of the stairwell wall.

Sweat cascaded from Deckard's forehead. The doorbell tolled a death knell through the small apartment. Deckard's tongue was like sandpaper

nd he cleared his throat to croak, "It's unlocked,
Mrs. Murdock; come on in."

The doorknob turned very slowly and the door
swung open just as slowly and Minnie Murdock
packed bulkily into Deckard's living room to ease
the door shut with great deliberation. Then she spun
to face him and she stood there smiling at him and
Deckard's blood turned to icy sludge because he
knew that smile and he knew Minnie Murdock. She
opened her shopping bag and she reached into it and
Lieutenant Kevin O'Hara rose from behind Deckard's big blue armchair. Minnie Murdock's lips
writhed into a wolverine snarl and she rummaged
frantically in the depths of her shopping bag and
there was the beginning of a hoarse shout of protest
before O'Hara shot her three times in the chest,
rapid-fire.

O'Hara returned his police special to its holster
and they crossed the room to stand at the feet of
the husky old woman spread-eagled motionless
on Deckard's living room floor. Contemptuously,
O'Hara kicked the shopping bag free of Minnie
Murdock's right arm. Clutched in her hand was a
Repentino-Morté Black Mamba Mark III with a
silencer screwed to its barrel. Her gray wig was
askew, her frosty-blue eyes glazing rapidly, and
Mike Madison was very dead.

O'Hara was shaking his head disapprovingly. He
said, "I went to see *Murder Times Seven* the other
night. In that performance the mayor dressed up
like an old woman and he wiped out the whole city
council in one fell fucking swoop." O'Hara struck a
wooden match with his thumbnail. He held it to a
cigarette and smoke curled from his nostrils. He
said, "Did you happen to see that particular version?"

Deckard shook his head.

O'Hara said, "Well, not to be critical, you understand, but that old-woman gimmick works a helluva lot better on East Adams Street than it does on Miriam Avenue."

You could have covered the three holes in Madison's chest with a railroad watch.

53

It had been the coldest, loneliest bed of Deckard's life. He sat up, bathed in one of his Guadalcanal sweats, groping blindly for the Chesterfields on the nightstand. There was big thunder rolling in from the west; prolonged chains of lightning stained his bedroom shades pale blue, and a snarling rain clawed at the windows. He found his cigarettes, jammed one into a corner of his mouth, put a match to it, and felt the smoke stall in his throat.

An hour later the rain slackened, then stopped, and the first welcome streaks of dawn grayed the room. Reality was setting in. He'd been fortunate. She was gone and it was over. She'd stumbled into his arms and tiptoed silently out of his life, but Deckard knew that he had yet to feel the full impact of the best thing that would ever happen to him, his loss of Heather Ralston.

But it would come, probably in the night. It would come just as surely as the Japanese had come to Bloody Ridge.

54

If it hadn't been for Lieutenant Kevin O'Hara and his scrawny bartender, the Lavender Lounge would have been empty. Deckard swung onto the bar stool next to O'Hara's and O'Hara turned slowly in Deckard's direction, taking out his notebook and consulting it. He said, "All right, Deckard, this is what we have. Last night, while I was with you, Shakey Lenkowski fucked up my cash register; he busted a quart of Chivas Regal; he rolled a keg of Old Washensachs beer over Lucille Wallingduck's left foot; he showed his pistol to some Puerto Rican and the damn thing went off and blew a hole in my jukebox, this being just before the Puerto Rican grabbed the gun and held the joint up to the tune of almost three hundred dollars." O'Hara took a deep breath and turned a notebook page. He said, "There's more."

Deckard said, "Stow it. Did you find her?"

O'Hara nodded and put his notebook away. He said, "Yeah, we found her. She was right where you said she'd be, at the Green Mill Tavern on Armitage Avenue, selling her keester at twenty-five a shot."

"How did she handle it?"

"Not badly, not badly at all. She seemed rather detached." Deckard waved to the bartender for drinks and O'Hara said, "Deckard, this is one very sick female."

"I know that now. I guess I always knew it. She plays games with people."

"It's worse than that. She plays games with her-*self*. Well, it just caught up with her. She's asked to be committed."

"Committed to where?"

"Gotta be Elgin."

"But that's a state facility! It's a fucking pigsty! Isn't there something better?"

"Oh, sure, there's Willow Haven, but it's private, it's expensive, and she's busted. Madison didn't leave her a dime. All of his money goes to the Guadalcanal Veterans Association."

"That figures. If Madison's in heaven, he's on a jungle island with mosquitos bigger than eagles, scorpions, dengue, yellow jaundice, jungle rot, malaria, and thirty thousand wild-eyed Japs, every damned one of them anxious to die for the Emperor."

"What if he's in hell?"

"Then there are no Japs."

The bartender poured Sunnybrook. They tossed them down and Deckard sat there, pushing his empty shot glass around, saying nothing. O'Hara studied him and said, "What's on your mind, Deckard?"

Deckard said, "Well, look, O'Hara, why didn't you say something when I showed her picture to you?"

"Should I have said something?"

"Damn right, you should have said something."

"What should I have said?"

248

"You should have told me that she was the hooker
ou fell in love with."

O'Hara caught the bartender's eye and pointed to
eir empty glasses. He said, "Well, Deckard, I
ought you two might have a straight-arrow ar-
ngement, and what the hell, almost everybody
eserves just one more chance. She was strange, of
urse; that was a big chunk of her appeal, but I saw
indications that she'd slipped her trolley. She
as just a loser named Holly Webster who told me
at she'd been a novice nun and that she'd grown
red of the grind. I could see that you were wild
out her and in such cases even your best friends
on't give you the right time of day. If I'd opened my
outh, you'd have knocked my teeth out."

Deckard shrugged. "All right, skip it. Was she
irprised to see you again?"

"She didn't remember me clearly. A year ago she
as peddling her ass out of here and she was
ending two or three nights a week with me at the
eridan Hotel; my wife committed suicide over her
October, and my God, Deckard, today she called
e *Phillip!*"

"She went from you to Madison?"

"I believe so."

"Doesn't *she* know?"

"Probably not."

"Who the hell *is* she? I mean *really.*"

"That's the spooky part. She's spent years slipping
and out of roles like some kind of chameleon.
e's lost track somewhere between there and
ere."

Deckard said, "Well, if she's asked to be commit-
d, she must be trying to come to grips with her-
lf."

249

"Too damned late, Deckard. She's locking tl
barn after she shot the horse."

"Was I mentioned?"

"Yes, and quite favorably, but you have to reali
that you're just another bush in the jungle of th
woman's mind. She enjoys the hell out of sex; sl
has the ability to feign high emotion; she appr
ciates romance with its subtle little intrigues—b
she doesn't possess the depth to really love som
one. She's in love with *love* and she's an emotion
masochist. She revels in secret sorrows. Lost lov
and all that purple mishmosh are like a drug to her

"Maybe it isn't quite that involved. Maybe she
been on the prowl for a fast jackpot."

O'Hara said, "No way! She had a shot at a jackp
with Madison and she blew him off and moved
with a hundred-dollar-a-day private gumshoe. N
she's too damned flighty to concentrate on that so
of campaign. She has a low threshold to boredor
Romance is her bag. She rides an affair to its zeni
and she bails out. She likes that big upsurge, but it
the fall that pleases her most. She has to have th
fall; it's like an orgasm for her, it gives her anoth
lost love to pine for. This tomato has so many lo
loves she can't get their names straight. *Philli*
Jesus Christ!"

"Gothic as hell."

"Sure, right out of a Victoria Holt smasher, but it
been expensive. She doesn't know whether her a
is punched or bored."

"Madison knew she was with me all the time"

"He knew in April. I talked to Jim Krakow
Keystone Investigations. Keystone will separa
pepper from fly manure if you can pay the freigl
and Madison could pay it. They found her for hi
twice. It took them a long time to track her from tl

250

Club Williwaw to the Lavender Lounge, but less than two weeks to locate her living with you. Then he turned the hounds onto your trail. He learned your occupation and that you dropped in at Mush's Teddy Bear Lounge a couple of times a week, and that was all he needed. He started frequenting Mush's, played some chess and cribbage, socialized with the boys, bought drinks and dropped hints, knowing that any inquiry regarding private detectives would lead to your office. Then he went to work creating an ironclad identity for a paper man."

Deckard said, "He turned in one helluva convincing job."

"He certainly did! As Harry Bishop, he rented an apartment and an office. As Bishop, he whistled up attention by advising the police of a threat on his life. As Bishop, he joined Casimar's Pistol Club, bought an excellent handgun, and qualified as Expert. As Bishop, he won a Greene Park chess tournament. He flew to Cleveland, stole an automobile, and drove it to Chicago where he cooked up a rubber bill of sale and a phony Minnie Murdock. Then he spotlighted the vehicle by sideswiping a Chicago squad car. He drove it to Garfield Boulevard where he abandoned it, leaving in it the bill of sale that established it as the property of Harry Bishop."

"It required some thought and some risks."

"Lots of thought, not too many risks. Meanwhile, he'd plucked a couple of actors out of the Friday night *Murder Times Seven* cast and he'd schooled them carefully in the roles they were to play in what he represented as being a harmless practical joke. DuKane was Boom-Boom LaTreuse, the ex-blues singer, and Drake was the telephone voice of Harry Bishop, the womanizing insurance agent. When the

stage was set, he hired you, knowing damned wel
that you'd play your cards close to the vest, tha
you'd say nothing about Bishop and DuKane. Wh
should you? A thousand bucks is a thousand bucks
He shot a hole in your window and he cat-and
moused you until he tired of the game. Then h
wiped out his cast to cover his tracks and prepare
to kill the bastard who'd stolen Dream Girl."

"The chess problem saved my ass."

"The chess problem was a symbolic thing, a
original. In it, Madison's emblem, a knight, ride
roughshod over a field in shambles. Also, it was a
out for Madison's peculiar brand of conscience. I
provided a wisp of the chivalrous ethic—give th
other guy a chance. He left you a message when h
stole that bishop. It was a thousand to one that you'
never catch its meaning, but he'd given you some
thing and that made everything kosher in Madison'
book."

Deckard said, "If I hadn't tumbled to the damne
thing Madison would have gotten away clean as
whistle with three murders."

"Deckard, there's just no way he could hav
missed! He'd breathed the breath of life into Harr
Bishop; there was no reasonable doubt of the exis
tence of a man by that name. 'Jealous Man Kills Ex
Girlfriend, Two Lovers, Vanishes!'—that woul
have been the headline! He'd have left that Blac
Mamba on your living room floor; we'd have traced i
through Casimar's Pistol Club to Harry Bishop; we'
have launched an all-out search for a man who'
never lived, and we'd still be looking when the roll i
called up yonder!"

"He could have made it simple. He could hav
strolled into my office one morning and shot m
between the eyes."

"No good. The woman was a common denominator nd we'd have gotten to him eventually; he knew at. No, it had to be Harry Bishop who took the rap. ver and above that, a simple murder would have ne nothing for Madison's ego. He was hopelessly visted, but he was brilliantly creative; he had to ove the pieces on the chess board and watch you llow a trail that led directly to yourself. In a sense, was playing God."

"Well, why not? He'd already played Judge and ry."

"Deckard, if Madison had been sane, he'd have ade a top-notch detective."

"If Madison had been sane, he wouldn't have been ladison."

O'Hara dug into a shirt pocket and placed a black hess bishop on the bar. "There's the pivot point, ur missing bishop. It was in Minnie Murdock's opping bag. You should frame it."

Deckard said, "The son of a bitch would have gutot me, sure as hell."

"That's not all. He'd have removed his wig and e'd have sat with you as you died, explaining all the elicious little intricacies of his master plot. It ould have been his finest hour."

"And all over what? A half-cracked floater I met on bridge last March!"

"Deckard, Madison was crazy about that floater, I ean wild-eyed *crazy*! She really had his number. le loved as only a psychopath can love and he hated s only a psychopath can hate. You had the woman ho'd rung his bell and he wanted your balls for at. With you out of the way he hoped to get her ack."

"He'd have had to hire Keystone Investigations

again. She was a few hours ahead of him. Do you think she knew?"

"That he planned to come for her? Possibly. There may have been contact."

"What the hell would have happened if Heather had been there and you weren't?"

"He'd have killed you. If she'd refused to come with him, he'd probably have killed *her*. Bishop would have picked up the tab." O'Hara got to his feet and said, "Well, Deckard, so much for the fucking twilight zone. I've been on my feet for more than twenty-four hours and I still have to go downtown and arrange a transfer."

"Transfer to where?"

"Straight back to narcotics. If I don't get away from Shakey Lenkowski, I'm gonna be out in the enchanted kingdom with our girlfriend."

They shook hands and Deckard said, "Thanks a million, O'Hara."

O'Hara said, "All in a day's work. Deckard, do yourself one helluva favor and forget her. By tomorrow she'll be throwing the make on one of the shrinks at Elgin."

Deckard shrugged. "I guess Madison knew her better than either of us. He told me that she was playing without all the face cards."

"Yeah, well, it takes one to know one." O'Hara spread his hands, palms up, in a helpless gesture. He said, "Why whip a dead donkey?" He started for the door, then came back to put a hand on Deckard's shoulder. He said, "You're still in love with her, suppose you know that."

Deckard said, "That makes two of us. You wanted Madison as badly as Madison wanted *me*! Christ, it was obvious! You didn't give him a *chance*!"

"He got a helluva lot better chance than he'd have
ven *you*."

"Yes, but for all you knew, that goddam shopping
ag was full of chocolate eclairs!"

O'Hara stood, silent for a moment, studying the
es of his scuffed black loafers. When he looked up,
ere were strange lights flickering deep in his dark,
oughtful eyes. He said, "See you around, Deck-
d."

With a great amount of admiration Deckard
atched Lieutenant Kevin O'Hara leave the Laven-
r Lounge.

The stalker who'd out-stalked the stalker.

55

The phone behind the bar was ringing and the scrawny bartender picked it up. He glanced in Deckard's direction and said, "Where did Kevin go?"

"Downtown, he told me."

The bartender nodded and talked briefly before hanging up. He was smiling. He said, "Well, Kevin just got lucky. They transferred his partner to another department."

"Lenkowski?"

"Yeah, they shipped his ass to narcotics."

Deckard's mind was a steel drum stuffed with pissed-off centipedes. He remained at the bar of the Lavender Lounge, blotting up double hookers of Sunnybrook and trying to tame his thoughts. The bartender gave him a wide berth, busying himself with the checking of a few invoices.

A light voice said, "Well, hi, there!" The chubby, cow-eyed auburn-haired hooker was braless under her sheer red blouse. She wore a short, white, pleated skirt and red pumps with four-inch heels. For a rather hefty gal she had excellent legs.

Deckard said, "Howdy."

She sat beside him and crossed her legs in slow, tantalizing fashion. She said, "I've seen you in here before. You were talking to Kevin the other day."

"Yes, we were reorganizing NATO."

"NATO. They make Shredded Wheat."

"No, you're thinking of NABISCO."

"So what's the difference?"

"I haven't the foggiest."

"My name's Yvonne; what's yours?"

"Mud, at the moment."

She laughed a musical little laugh. She said, "That's a nice name. Buy me a drink, Muddy?" Deckard made a sign to the bartender and Yvonne said, "Lonely?"

Deckard said, "Is a pig's ass pork?" He liked her eyes. There wasn't a great deal of intelligence in them, but they were big and soft and brown with a good-natured twinkle.

Yvonne smiled and slipped from her bar stool to move it in Deckard's direction. When she reseated herself, their knees were touching. She said, "By the way, Muddy, I go any route." She giggled. "Well, *almost*. I mean within reason, you understand."

Deckard said, "I understand. I'm a reasonable man. I come from a long line of missionaries."

Yvonne squeezed his arm. She said, "Well, my God, you wouldn't have to be *that* reasonable!"

The bartender brought Yvonne's drink, an old-fashioned minus the fruit. He picked up some of Deckard's change and moved clear of the negotiations. Deckard looked Yvonne over. He said, "What's the tariff?"

"Twenty for plenty."

"I'm not hep to the market. Is that a good shake?"

"It's the buy of the century! My gosh, Holly

Webster was getting twenty-five more than a year ago!"

"Maybe Holly Webster was worth twenty-five."

"Not really. Holly was a novelty item. She'd been a novice nun. Men get all turned on by taking a novice nun to bed. Especially Catholic men. This is a Catholic neighborhood. Holly made a whole pile of money."

Deckard didn't say anything.

Yvonne said, "You ever take a novice nun to bed?"

"I doubt it."

"Well, they're no different than the rest of us. I mean they don't douche with holy water and there's no halo around it or anything like that."

Deckard said, "How much for all night?"

Yvonne said, "We might discuss it over dinner. There's a discount that goes with dinner."

"Really?"

"Yes, but only if vodka martinis are included."

"Got to have vodka martinis."

Yvonne put her hand on Deckard's leg. It was a friendly hand, dimpled and very warm. She said, "As soon as we finish our drinks, okay, Muddy?"

To hell with his nobility. She was no Heather Ralston, but on this particular evening he'd have gone to bed with Medusa.

56

Low frothy-black clouds tumbled eastward. A pale-gold afternoon sun struggled ineffectually to pierce ashen skies. A huge flight of crows flapped hurriedly into the north. The private road was long, winding, and bordered on either hand by barren weeping willows. Deckard parked his Olds in the small blacktopped lot, got out, and permitted a raw March wind to sweep him toward the ancient red-brick building. The sign over the arched entrance was black, lettered in gold. WILLOW HAVEN, A PLACE OF PEACE.

The nurse at the desk was well into her fifties. She wore a pince-nez and she was crisply efficient, the type that Deckard had always associated with a pince-nez. She glanced at her watch and said, "Mr. Deckard, you are her first visitor and we don't want to upset her, do we?"

Deckard said, "Certainly not."

"Then limit your visit to one-half hour or less, please." Deckard nodded and she escorted him part-way down an immaculate, antiseptic-smelling hall. She opened a door.

Deckard stepped into the room. It was small, dim, silent, and sparsely furnished. There was a bed neatly made, a tiny desk with wilted roses in a tall white vase, and a dark-blue upholstered chair. Heather Ralston sat unmoving, staring out at the panorama of gray March sky. She wore a powder-blue flannel wrapper and black corduroy scuffs. Her hand lay limply on the arm of the chair and Deckard touched it gently. She looked up with dull green eyes. She'd lost about ten pounds. Her face was narrow now, her lips pale and cracked, her copper-gold hair streaked with slender rivulets of gray. She said, "Buzz? Buzzer, is that you?"

Deckard said, "Yes, it's me."

After a moment she said, "Dear God, Buzz, I'm so terribly *sorry!*" Her voice was smaller and more hoarse then he'd ever heard it.

He said, "Forget it; it's behind you." He pulled a spindly-legged chair away from the desk and sat on it gingerly, dropping his hat to the highly polished hardwood floor. He said, "How are you?"

"Better, they keep telling me."

"Yes, I've been calling."

"I've had bad nights, Buzz; more than a few."

"They're in the past. Don't dwell on the past, think about today."

"Over six months in this place . . ." Her voice trailed away.

"It'll end. All things end."

"Do they?"

"Trust me. I'm an authority on the subject."

She licked her dry lips. "Everything was so fuzzy when I was transferred here from Elgin. . . . It's clearing now, just a bit, but only in spots. . . . I've had several personalities, some of which were whores. . . ." She smiled wryly. "I seemed to gravitate to that profession."

"Can you recall having been a novice nun?"

"No, but I must have been . . . sometimes the prayers and the routines come to me very vividly. . . . Buzz, this is like trying to climb out of midnight . . . but they seem to think that my internal self-helper will lead me to daylight eventually."

"Your internal self-helper?"

"That's what the doctors call my identity with the fewest loose screws."

"Tell me about your internal self-helper. What's she like?"

"You know her. . . . She lived with you . . . your luck of the draw, I guess."

"Heather Ralston? Was Heather real?"

"As real as any of the others. . . . I liked Heather. . . . Buzz, there were so many men . . . if you count customers, maybe thousands."

Deckard said, "No more of that! *Today*, not *yesterday*!"

"I just wanted to say that my memory flickers, but I remember you first, Buzz . . . first and best . . . do you know why?"

"I haven't the foggiest."

"Because there was an honest kindness about you . . . you wanted nothing from me but *me*. . . . a woman hardly ever finds that kind of love."

"Being kind to Heather Ralston was the easiest thing I've ever done."

"You did it well . . . those were happy days . . . the happiest of my life . . . then I became Corkie Henderson again."

"Again? These personalities . . . they repeat?"

"Oh, yes, but it's a very uneven cycle."

"You've been Heather Ralston before?"

263

"No, just once, that was with you. I'd like to be Heather all of the time. When did we break up, Buzz?"

"September."

"Last September?"

"Yes."

"Did we quarrel?"

"No, you just packed up and checked out."

"That was Corkie Henderson." She was gazing through the window, her teeth clenching her lower lip. She'd retained that characteristic, even during her conversion to Corkie Henderson. She said, "I have some kind of schizophrenia . . . *schizophrenia* is a euphemism for 'bats in the belfry'. . . . I'm *nuts*, Buzz; it's just that damned simple."

Deckard frowned. He said, "Look, schizophrenia is no big deal! Chicago's *full* of schizophrenics! Why, you have to be a certified schizophrenic to qualify for an Illinois driver's license! Look at the bright side of the coin! What the hell, you aren't foaming at the mouth and screaming "Jesus, Jesus, Jesus,' are you?"

"Not yet, but who does *that*?"

"My cousin, for one."

"Is he a schizophrenic?"

"No, she's a Pentecostal."

She smiled. "God, Buzzer, you're a tonic!"

"Get one thing through your head! You're going to be all right!"

"Not until I find reality. . . . Buzz, where the hell is reality?" There was so much of the lost little girl about her now.

Deckard said, "Probably somewhere near the middle, Heather; who really knows?"

She shook her head. "Not Heather, Buzz . . . and not Boom-Boom or Holly or Corkie or God knows

ow many others. . . . It's Annette . . . Annette
Vilkinson from Cedar Rapids, Iowa. . . . Annette's
n orphan . . . her parents were alcoholics who
rank themselves to death. I'm progressing, you
ee."

"I'm sorry about your parents." He meant it. He
urned to glance at the drooping roses on the desk
ehind him. He said, "Your flowers aren't doing too
vell."

"No, sometimes it gets awfully warm in here . . .
ut thank you so much . . . they mean a great deal
o me. . . . I've pressed one in a book . . . Long-
ellow's 'Song of Hiawatha.'"

Deckard picked up his hat and stood. He placed
is hand on Annette Wilkinson's gray-streaked cop-
er-gold hair. He tilted her head and leaned to kiss
er faded, cracked lips. He reached into his coat
ocket and placed the tiny gift-wrapped bottle of
'everie by François Carrieré in the lap of her
owder-blue wrapper. He said, "See you."

A tall man was coming up the hallway. He wore a
umpled dark-blue suit; he had an oversize nose, a
eet-red face, and quick, bright eyes; he walked
vith the stilted gait of a Hialeah flamingo. He
pproached with a smile, extending his hand. "Mr.
eckard, it's a pleasure! It is Mr. Deckard, isn't it?"

Deckard said, "Yes, why?"

"I'd heard that you'd be in and I saw you leaving
er room. She speaks of you often. Mr. Deckard, I'm
r. Frederick Nesbitt, Willow Haven's resident
sychiatrist. It was thoughtful of you to drop by."

"I've been trying to 'drop by' for six months. She
an't take telephone calls and this is the first time
ve been allowed within shooting distance of the
lace. I believe the word is *incommunicado*."

Dr. Nesbitt sighed. "Yes, Mr. Deckard, you must

understand that the first months are rather touch
and-go. We thought it best that Becky try to worl
some of this out on her own, free of outside influ
ences."

Deckard said, "Hold it! *Becky*?"

"Yes, Becky Collingsworth. We refer to her a
Becky Collingsworth."

Deckard grinned. He said, "Sorry, Doc; righ
horse, wrong stall. I was visiting Annette Wilkir
son."

Dr. Nesbitt said, "You aren't familiar with Beck
Collingsworth?"

"Never heard of her."

"You will, Mr. Deckard, and quite soon. Beck
Collingsworth's around the next corner. She's fro
Manitowoc, Wisconsin, and we think we're going t
like her. She's a pleasant, quiet sort; she reads a lo
and she can quote lengthy passages of 'Hiawath;
from memory. Amazing retention!"

Deckard blinked. He said, "Let's try it agair
You've left me at the post."

Dr. Nesbitt took a deep breath. "Well, you se
Mr. Deckard, we're hoping that Becky Collings
worth is the one we've been waiting for, the re
woman in the room you just left. Right now we'r
dealing with Annette Wilkinson, but Annette
showing us occasional flashes of Becky . . . pr
views, in a sense."

Deckard's scalp was prickling. He peered at D
Nesbitt and said, "She isn't Annette Wilkinson?"

"We thought she was, but she isn't. Unless we'r
misreading her signals, Annette will be leaving
shortly."

"But you infer that she may not be Becky Colling
worth, either."

"It's a fifty-fifty shot, certainly no better than that."

"And is she isn't Becky Collingsworth, there will be others?"

"Undoubtedly."

"How *many* others, for Christ's sake?"

"Who can say? One or two, possibly *dozens*. This is a very deep well, Mr. Deckard, perhaps the deepest I've ever encountered."

"How will you know when you've struck bottom?"

"We won't. We'll *never* know. Her past has been completely obliterated. She's on no missing persons lists and she isn't wanted by the authorities anywhere in the country. We can only hope that she'll stabilize at a decent identity, and in the opinion of Willow Haven's staff, Becky Collingsworth shows signs of being acceptable."

"But you really won't know if she's Becky Collingsworth or Lucretia Borgia?"

"That's a shade on the strong side but accurate, in essence."

"If she levels off at Becky Collingsworth, will there be any assurances that she won't become someone else later in the ball game?"

"None whatsoever. This is a classic case of schizophrenia, multiple-choice style. She might maintain an even keel for years, then change identities three times in a week."

Deckard said, "A time bomb."

"Well put. She could go off at any moment and you'd never know what triggered her. Where older women are concerned, we have a tendency to attribute sudden drastic personality alterations to menopause, but in *this* case . . ." Dr. Nesbitt shook his head and shrugged.

Deckard said, "But in *this* case you haven't the foggiest."

"That's right, Mr. Deckard, we haven't the foggiest."

In the lobby the nurse at the desk crooked an authoritative finger at him and he walked over to her. She was scowling at a thick gray ledger. She adjusted her pince-nez and cleared her throat. She said, "Mr. Deckard, you're more than three weeks in arrears."

Deckard said, "The check's in the mail."

The nurse closed the ledger and smiled a prim, proper smile. She said, "Thank you, Mr. Deckard! Have a nice day! The sun peeked out for a moment during your visit. Pity it couldn't have stayed with us."

Deckard said, "Yes."

When he left the building, the sky was charcoal, a cold rain was falling, and the March wind was harsh on his face.

MORE MYSTERIOUS PLEASURES

HAROLD ADAMS
THE NAKED LIAR
When a sexy young widow is framed for the murder of her husband, Carl Wilcox comes through to help her fight off cops and big-city goons.
#420 $3.95

EARL DERR BIGGERS
THE HOUSE WITHOUT A KEY
Charlie Chan debuts in the Honolulu investigation of an expatriate Bostonian's murder.
#421 $3.95

JAMES M. CAIN
THE ENCHANTED ISLE
A beautiful runaway is involved in a deadly bank robbery in this posthumously published novel.
#415 $3.95

WILLIAM DeANDREA
THE LUNATIC FRINGE
Police Commissioner Teddy Roosevelt and Officer Dennis Muldoon comb 1896 New York for a missing exotic dancer who holds the key to the murder of a prominent political cartoonist.
#306 $3.95

DICK FRANCIS
THE SPORT OF QUEENS
The autobiography of the celebrated race jockey/crime novelist.
#410 $3.95

JOHN GARDNER
THE GARDEN OF WEAPONS
Big Herbie Kruger returns to East Berlin to uncover a double agent. He confronts his own past and life's only certainty—death.
#103 $4.50

JOE GORES
A TIME OF PREDATORS
When Paula Halstead kills herself after witnessing a horrid crime, her husband vows to avenge her death. Winner of the Edgar Allan Poe Award.
#215 $3.95

BRIAN GARFIELD
DEATH WISH

Paul Benjamin is a modern-day New York vigilante, stalking the rapist-killers who victimized his wife and daughter. The basis for the Charles Bronson movie. #301 $3.95

DEATH SENTENCE

A riveting sequel to DEATH WISH. The action moves to Chicago as Paul Benjamin continues his heroic (or is it psychotic?) mission to make city streets safe. #302 $3.95

TRIPWIRE

A crime novel set in the American West of the late 1800s. Boag, a black outlaw, seeks revenge on the white cohorts who crossed him and left him for dead. "One of the most compelling characters in recent fiction"—Robert Ludlum. #303 $3.95

FEAR IN A HANDFUL OF DUST

Four psychiatrists, three men and a woman, struggle across the blazing Arizona desert—pursued by a fanatic killer they themselves have judged insane. "Unique and disturbing"—Alfred Coppel. #304 $3.95

NAT HENTOFF
BLUES FOR CHARLIE DARWIN

Gritty, colorful Greenwich Village sets the scene for Noah Green and Sam MacKibbon, two street-wise New York cops who are as at home in the Village's jazz clubs as they are at a homicide scene. #208 $3.95

THE MAN FROM INTERNAL AFFAIRS

Detective Noah Green wants to know who's stuffing corpses into East Village garbage cans . . . and who's lying about him to the Internal Affairs Division. #409 $3.95

PATRICIA HIGHSMITH
THE BLUNDERER

An unhappy husband attempts to kill his wife by applying the murderous methods of another man. When things go wrong, he pays a visit to the more successful killer—a dreadful error. #305 $3.95

ELMORE LEONARD
THE HUNTED

Long out of print, this 1974 novel by the author of *Glitz* details the attempts of a man to escape killers from his past. #401 $3.95

MR. MAJESTYK

Sometimes bad guys can push a good man too far, and when that good guy is a Special Forces veteran, everyone had better duck. #402 $3.95

THE BIG BOUNCE

Suspense and black comedy are cleverly combined in this tale of a dangerous drifter's affair with a beautiful woman out for kicks. #403 $3.95

STUART KAMINSKY'S "TOBY PETERS" SERIES

NEVER CROSS A VAMPIRE
When Bela Lugosi receives a dead bat in the mail, Toby tries to catch the prankster. But Toby's time is at a premium because he's also trying to clear William Faulkner of a murder charge!   #107 $3.95

HIGH MIDNIGHT
When Gary Cooper and Ernest Hemingway come to Toby for protection, he tries to save them from vicious blackmailers.   #106 $3.95

HE DONE HER WRONG
Someone has stolen Mae West's autobiography, and when she asks Toby to come up and see her sometime, he doesn't know how deadly a visit it could be.   #105 $3.95

BULLET FOR A STAR
Warner Brothers hires Toby Peters to clear the name of Errol Flynn, a blackmail victim with a penchant for young girls. The first novel in the acclaimed Hollywood-based private eye series.   #308 $3.95

THE FALA FACTOR
Toby comes to the rescue of lady-in-distress Eleanor Roosevelt, and must match wits with a right-wing fanatic who is scheming to overthrow the U.S. Government.   #309 $3.95

ED MCBAIN

SNOW WHITE AND ROSE RED
A beautiful heiress confined to a sanitarium engages Matthew Hope to free her—and her $650,000.   #414 $3.95

PETER O'DONNELL

MODESTY BLAISE
Modesty and Willie Garvin must protect a shipment of diamonds from a gentleman about to murder his lover and an *un*civilized sheik.   #216 $3.95

SABRE TOOTH
Modesty faces Willie's apparent betrayal and a modern-day Genghis Khan who wants her for his mercenary army.   #217 $3.95

A TASTE FOR DEATH
Modesty and Willie are pitted against a giant enemy in the Sahara, where their only hope of escape is a blind girl whose time is running out.   #218 $3.95

I, LUCIFER
Some people carry a nickname too far . . . like the maniac calling himself Lucifer. He's targeted 120 souls, and Modesty and Willie find they have a personal stake in stopping him.   #219 $3.95

THE IMPOSSIBLE VIRGIN
Modesty fights for her soul when she and Willie attempt to rescue an albino girl from the evil Brunel, who lusts after the secret power of an idol called the Impossible Virgin.   #220 $3.95

DAVID WILLIAMS' "MARK TREASURE" SERIES
UNHOLY WRIT
London financier Mark Treasure helps a friend reacquire some property. He stays to unravel the mystery when a Shakespeare manuscript is discovered and foul murder done. **#112 $3.95**

TREASURE BY DEGREES
Mark Treasure discovers there's nothing funny about a board game called "Funny Farms." When he becomes involved in the takeover struggle for a small university, he also finds there's nothing funny about murder. **#113 $3.95**